DEADWORLD™
ZOMBIE SODA

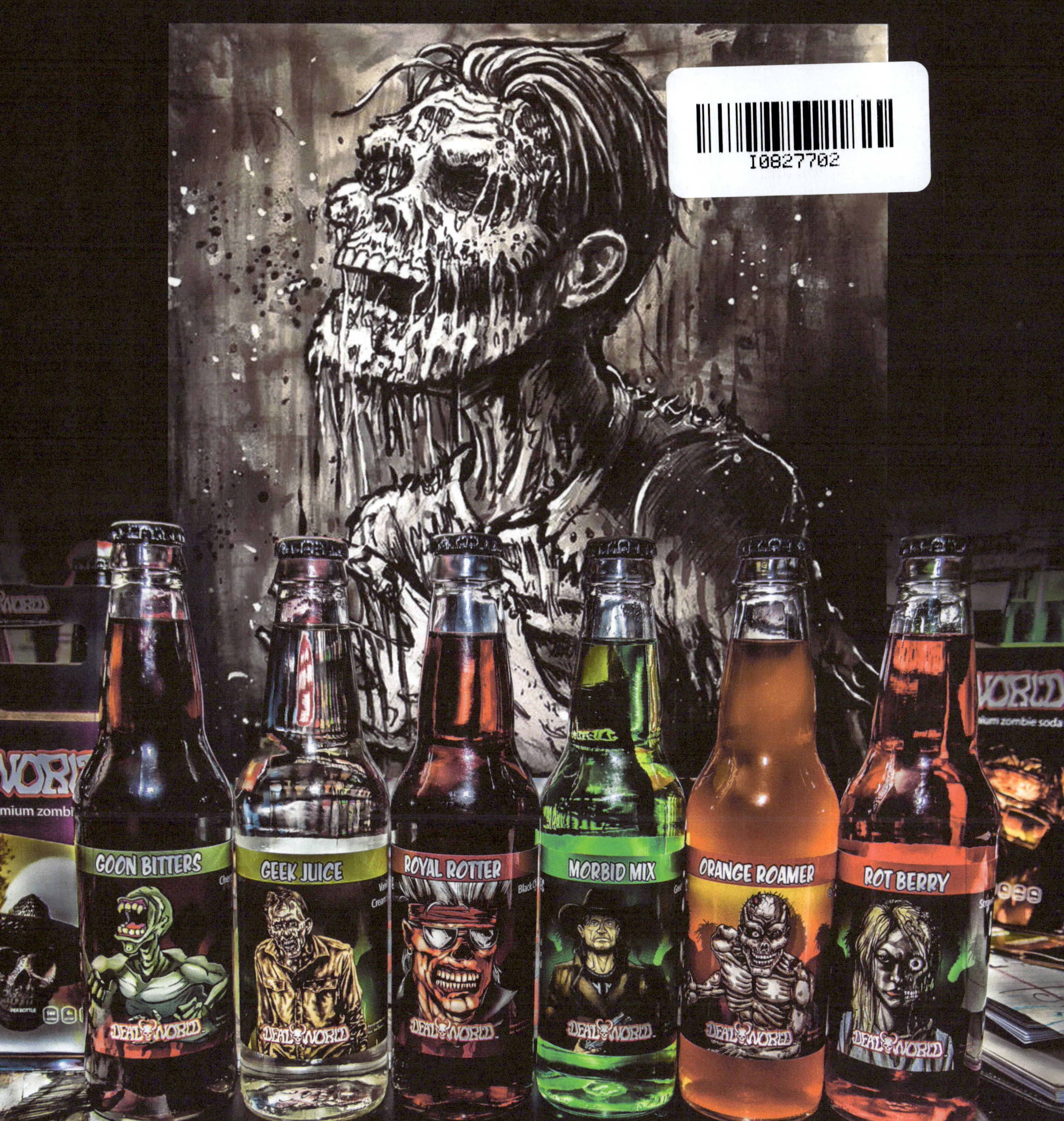

I0827702

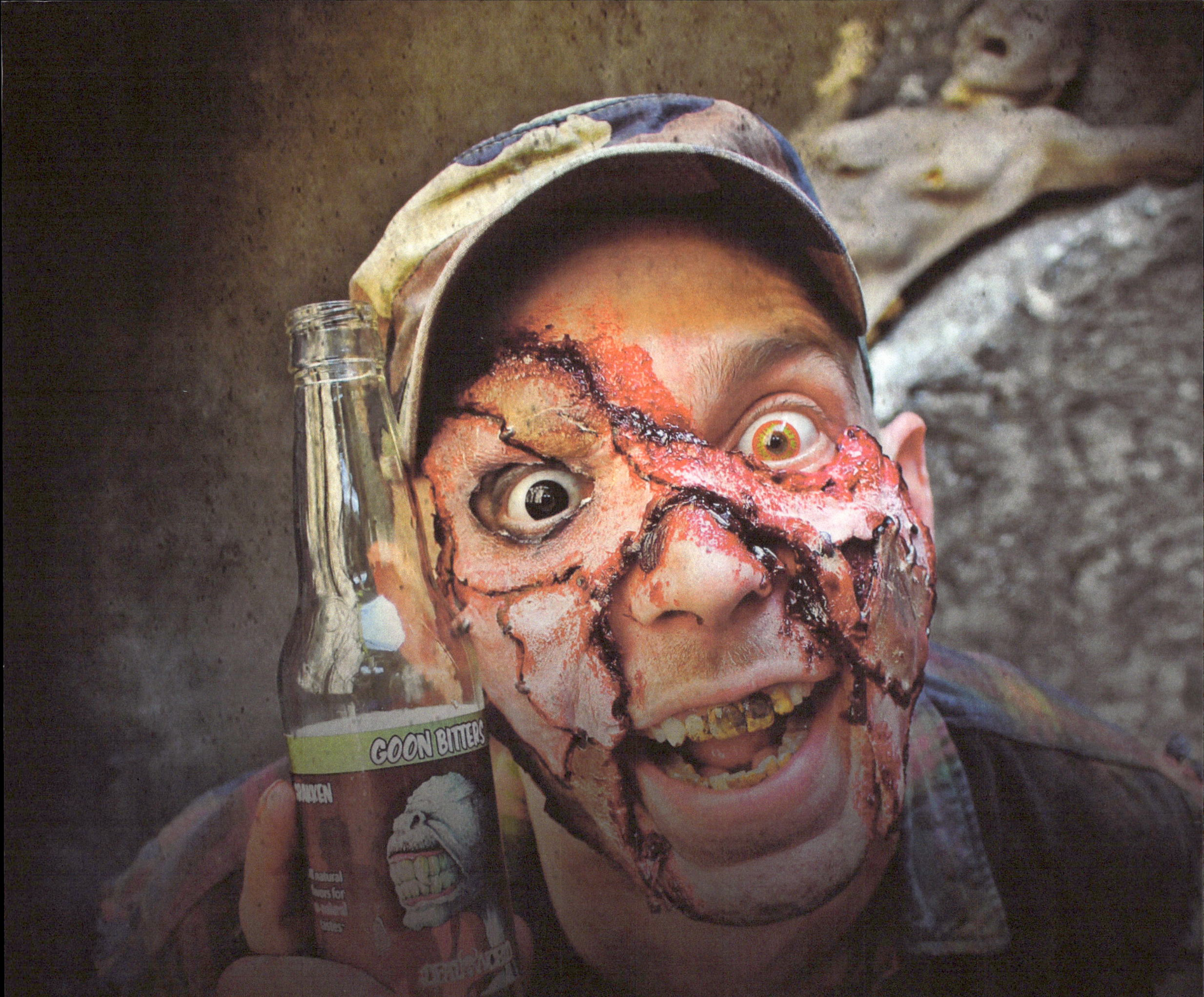

WRITTEN AND COMPILED BY PAUL BURKE

EDITED BY JOSHUA WERNER & PAUL BURKE

DESIGNED BY JOSHUA WERNER

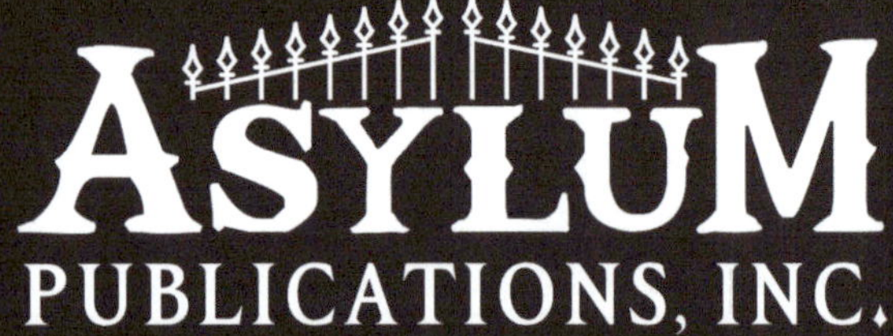

Distributed by 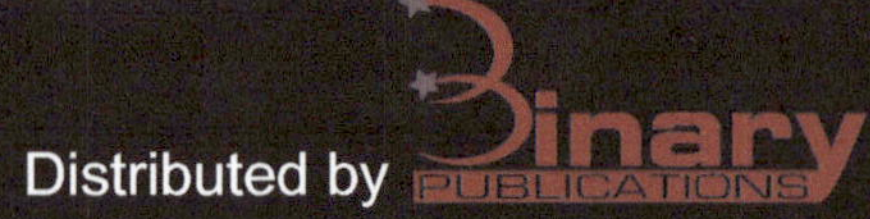

CEO AND EDITOR IN CHIEF PAUL BURKE

CREATIVE DIRECTOR JOSHUA WERNER

ISBN: 978-1-7339309-0-1

DeadWorld Zombie Soda™. Published by Asylum Publications, Inc.™ All photos are © by their respective photographers. Asylum Pulications, Inc.™ and DeadWorld™ are TM. All rights reserved. No portion of this publication may be reproduced or transmitted, in any form by any means, without written consent from the Publisher, except for any small excerpts for the purpose of review. For further information regarding custom photo/art books, ordering wholesale, or other inquiries, please write to asylumpublications75@gmail.com.

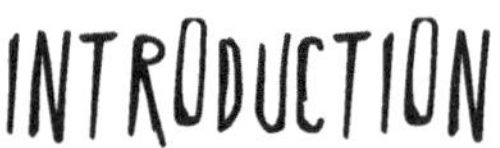

INTRODUCTION

After a long entrepreneurial career publishing prints, comic books, trade books, producing videos and co-founding TMP International (McFarlane Toys) in 1993, I sold out of TMP International in 1999 and pursued other traditional business ventures and advising. In December of 2013 I visited a soda bottling plant in Detroit, Michigan on a discovery assignment. I brought Bill Martin, the retired President of McFarlane Toys along to assist before he returned to Florida.

During the plant walkthrough Bill said to me, "too bad you didn't know about this – you would have sold a million bottles of Spawn soda" and I said "you're right".

I was still publishing an occasional book with Gary Reed, a longtime friend and partner for twenty+ years and mentioned Bill's visit and what he said during the walkthrough and Gary said, "he still owned the DeadWorld comic book, for "fun" why don't we make some soda with DeadWorld – we haven't made any products in ten years".

We had zero experience with soda so we teamed up with the bottling company I had visited for their expertise and together agreed to produce a line of twelve flavors of premium cane sugar soda pop with the DeadWorld theme. Gary and I decided to produce a collector version of each flavor. Our goal was to produce about 300 cases of each flavor, sell them to collectors through Diamond Distributors and that was the end. It was to be a fun project.

We selected twelve flavors from traditional flavors; root beer and strawberry to specialty flavors; Green Apple and Cotton Candy and everything in between.

We brought Jim Blakeslee in as our graphic designer and web/media expert. Gary worked with Jim to create a theme approach to the label design. The labels featured characters and names from DeadWorld featuring zombies to zombie hunters with zombie theme titles for the flavors. Then Gary engaged forty-eight comic book artists to design labels and four packs.

The crowns (bottle caps) were designed to have primarily the DeadWorld name on the top with limited amount of skulls on the cap. The interior of the caps featured "Caprice", the company name with limited runs of pentagrams, skulls and hands from the grave. There are 384 possible variations of soda pop in the soda line.

We then designed collector four pack carriers for each flavor, cases and a collector box designed to hold a bottle of each soda flavor with a small comic book.

Our first run of soda was on November 12th, 2014 just in time for our scheduled launch party at Wyndham Gardens, a pool resort in Sterling Heights, Michigan on the 20th.

Gary and I invited the 48 artists, friends, family, people who worked on the project and a few reporters we knew expecting a turnout of about 60 people. Well over 100 invited people attended. We had brought 100 cases of soda for the event and after a few hours we opened the doors to the guests of the hotel and another 100 people came in to the event. At the end of the night everything was gone except a few thousand empty soda bottles.

During the event, Janelle Burke Powers said the soda was really popular, we should keep the business going and she would work for us. Gary and I decided to keep it going and see where it went. The rest is history.

The company started getting product placement in a few stores in the Detroit area in early 2015. We started doing product demos in stores in late March. The first store, Hollywood Market wanted a safe demo, one without a zombie character. We brought in the comic book artist Josh Werner to do zombie sketches. Hollywood sold 23 cases of soda that month, an impressive amount, considering premium sodas normally sell between 3 and 5 cases of soda, per store, per month.

In April of 2015, we did our first convention, Motor City Nightmares. At the event I was introduced to Eric Reichert, Gary's partner in Caliber Comics. Eric joined Caprice Brands as a partner and outside sales director.

Through Eric's efforts we started shipping samples and promotion material to several grocery chains and beverage distributors. By June we were selling and shipping numerous "in-and-out" orders to grocery stores for test sales and picking up small distributors for resale. We were getting interest, no retailer was sure how the product would sell, but everyone was intrigued. The sales kept growing.

At this time, we caught the interest of a Kroger national C-store buyer, Joe Knox and a few national distributors. While not buyers of DeadWorld Zombie Soda immediately, they provided us with invaluable advice and encouragement moving forward.

Shortly after Motor City Nightmare we were introduced to new groups of people in the "haunt" business, this quickly expanded to people in "steam punk", "underground music" and "custom cars". These relationships provided DeadWorld Zombie Soda with lots of promotion and hundreds of photographs from around the world from DeadWorld Zombie Soda photoshoots.

In September of 2015 we released the DeadWorld Zombie potato chips made by Better Made to great success. The fans loved the chips and while stores reluctantly handled the chips during Halloween, we sold out at retail.

Bonnie Brown, a photographer from Ohio led a group from the Haunted Hydro in numerous photo sessions, leading to our discovery of Jeff Joslyn (Zombie Jeff), one of the best multi-character zombies who did live zombie promotions for us in the Midwest and Eric Littlefield used many of the models from Gorgeous Girls in photo sessions to promote the soda.

Charlie Hayes introduced us to Robert Richards who created great photo shoots in Florida for promotion and the DeadWorld calendar and Catherine Moon organized a photo session in Amsterdam featuring DeadWorld Zombie Soda.

Carol Moraca started promoting DeadWorld Zombie Soda through her custom, haunted cars that she was building in Las Vegas and the horrorcore rap group, Twiztid went further with co-branded Twiztid soda labels.

As part of the promotion efforts, we produced a series of trading cards and posters and sold the sodas at comic book and horror conventions to generate consumer interest. The most notable convention was Planet Comic Con in Kansas City. We sold a four pack of soda every 53 seconds during a three day convention.

Freddie Novack and Heather Renee Nance made special appearances as zombies at the 2015 NACS convention for retailers and gas stations. These attractive ladies charmed everyone and definitely set the tone for 2016 sales.

In October, 2015 we did a Halloween trick-or-treat promotion at Holiday Market in Canton, Michigan with Dedd Fredd, a well-known, classic zombie actor as the DeadWorld zombie. The event attracted over 500 families over a two hour period with children dressed in costume. It was a great success and Dedd Fredd became one of the featured zombies of DeadWorld as we moved ahead.

2016 had impressive growth with sales in approximately 30 states and Canada. The company sold very well in Ohio, Indiana and Illinois during 2016 in major independent retailers, small chains and distributors purchasing soda on a regular basis.

In July, 2016 our sales reps set up a DeadWorld Zombie Soda display at a show for Jewel-Osco Store Managers in Chicago. This show un-expectedly led to initial orders for thousands of cases of soda, 60 to 120 cases per store to be sold during the months of September and October.

Janelle Powers scheduled zombie sampling events for thirty stores featuring Chicago area zombie characters, primarily Kevin and Bonnie Biksacky. The events went extremely well and the stores had 100% sell through.

At the same time, a distributor decided to test the soda at Hy-Vee Stores in Iowa and Nebraska by placing over a thousand cases, 20 to 30 cases per store, in select Hy-Vee Stores during September / October and had 100% sell through without zombie promotions.

CVS Michigan came on board and placed a few cases per store in Michigan order to test during October and had sell through as well.

However, we unfortunately lost Gary Reed on October 3rd, 2016. Gary's passing at the height of this activity and growth was a major setback both personally and professionally when we needed him. Gary and I had set out to achieve a goal… "Have fun", we accomplished that and more, we created a significant brand. However, the fun was gone and the team decided to close the company, Caprice Brands and retire DeadWorld Zombie Soda at the end of 2016.

In 2018, Eric Reichert, the DeadWorld IP owner, brought DeadWorld Zombie Soda and an energy drink back to market. I hope it continues to grow.

- Paul Burke,
CEO, Asylum Books

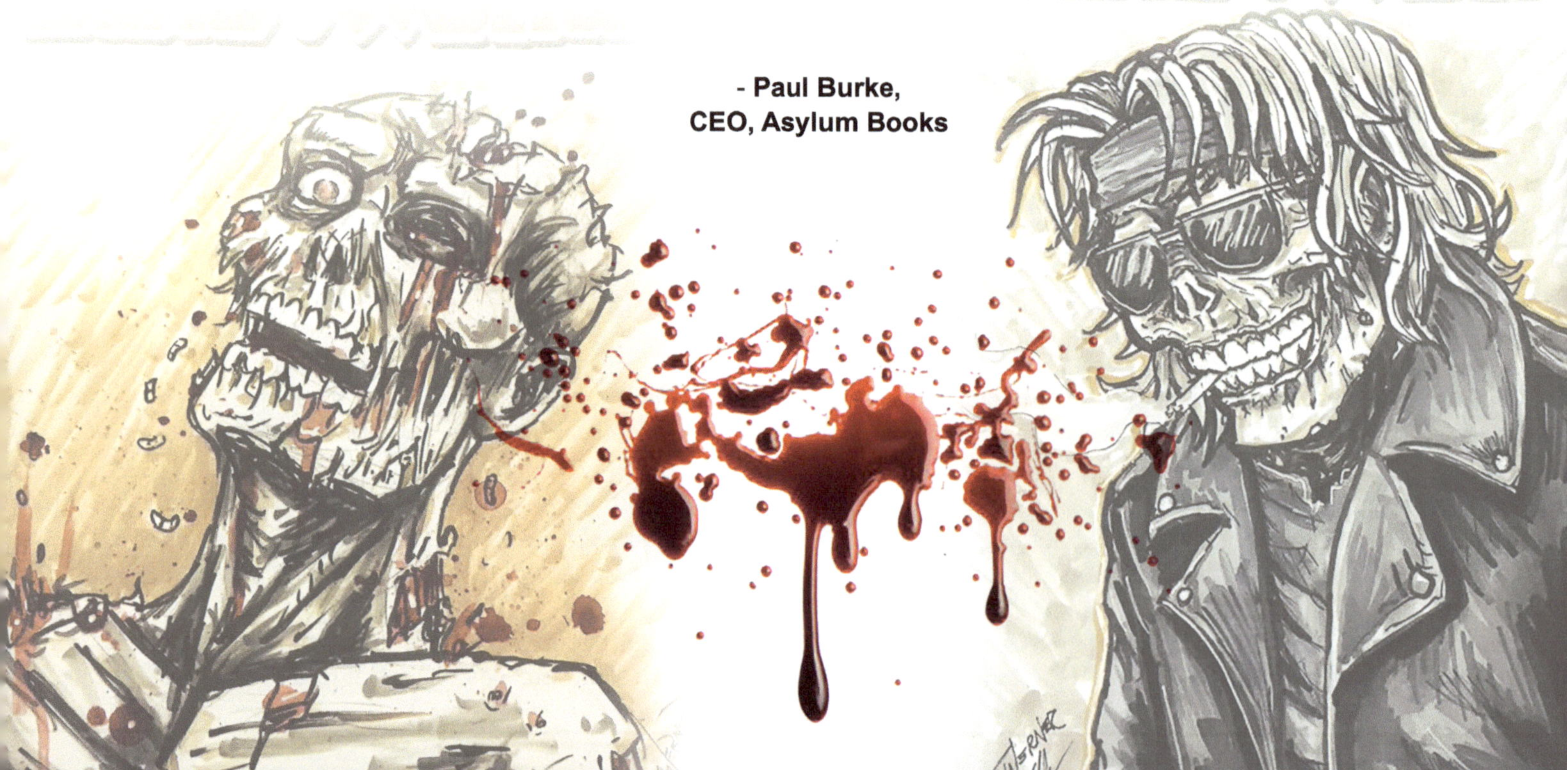

BLACK CHERRY

BLACK CHERRY

Royal Rotter

Horrifyingly Good

All natural flavors for **un-natural** tastes™

DEADWORLD

PREMIUM

ZOMBIE SODA®

Based on the Deadworld comic book.
Art: Vince Locke

Nutrition Facts

Service Size
1 Bottle (355mL)

Amount Per Serving
Calories 144

	% Daily Value*
Total Fat 0g	0%
Sodium 22mg	1%
Total Carbohydrate 38g	11%
Sugars 38g	
Protein 0g	

* Percent Daily Values are based on a 2,000 calorie diet.

INGREDIENTS: CARBONATED WATER, CANE SUGAR, CITRIC ACID, SODIUM BENZOATE (PRESERVATIVE), NATURAL FLAVORS, CARAMEL COLOR, RED 40, AND BLUE 1.

WWW.DEADWORLDZOMBIESODA.COM

Label #42

Bottled by Intrastate Distributors Inc. 20021 Exeter St, Detroit, MI 48203

CA CASH REFUND . CT . MA . VT . NY . ME . IA . OR .
HI 5¢ REFUND . MI 10¢ REFUND

Please Recycle

Caprice™

Caprice Brands and DeadWorld Beverages are trademarks of Caprice Brands, LLC.
DeadWorld is a trademark and copyright of Gary Reed and used with permission. All rights reserved.

CREAM SODA

CREAM SODA

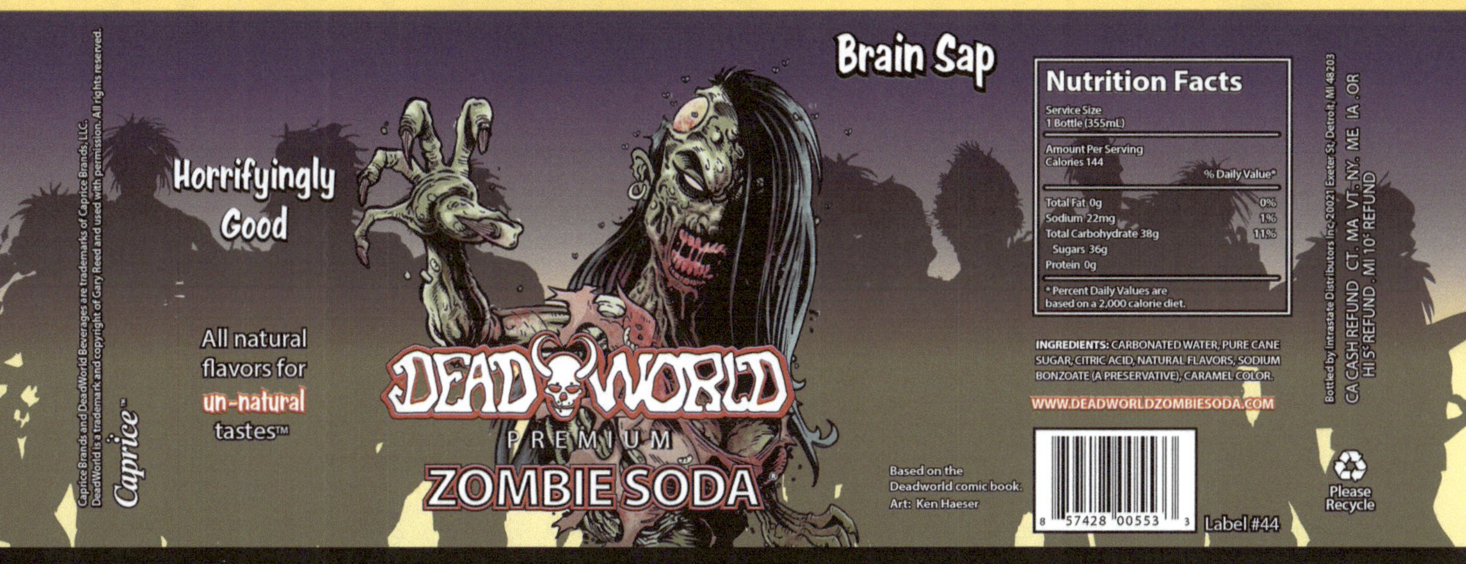

GREEN APPLE

GREEN APPLE

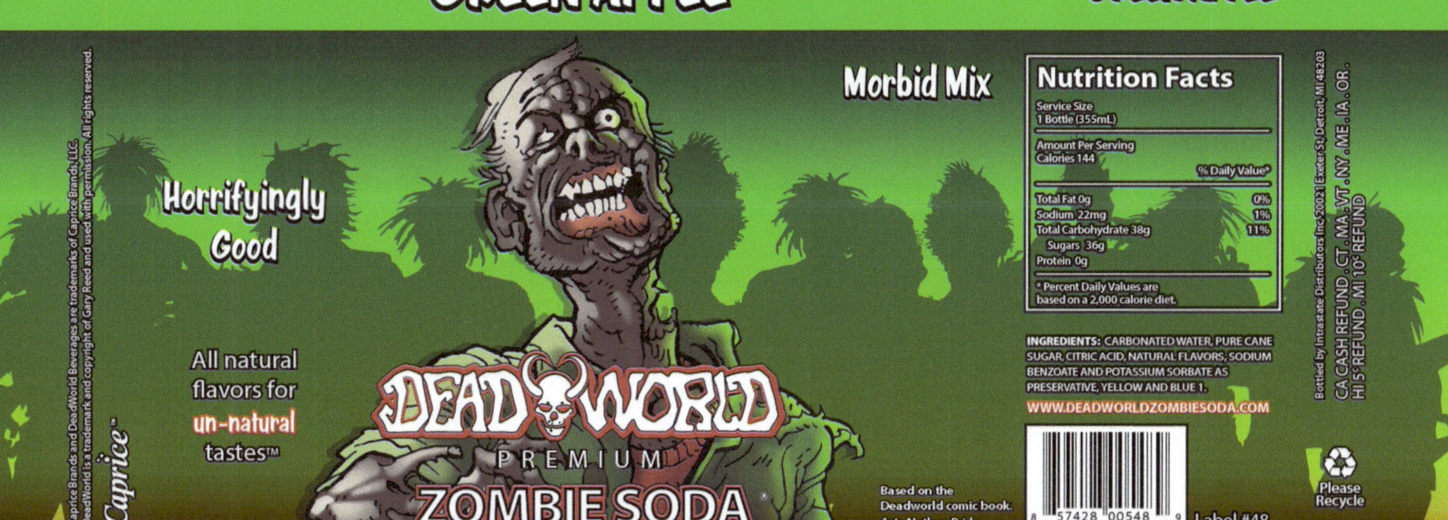

ROOT BEER

ROOT BEER

Caprice Brands and DeadWorld Beverages are trademarks of Caprice Brands, LLC. DeadWorld is a trademark and copyright of Gary Reed and used with permission. All rights reserved.

Caprice™

Horrifyingly Good

All natural flavors for un-natural tastes™

DEADWORLD PREMIUM ZOMBIE SODA®

Twilight Shuffler

Based on the Deadworld comic book.
Art: Dalibor Talajic

Nutrition Facts

Service Size
1 Bottle (355mL)

Amount Per Serving
Calories 144

	% Daily Value*
Total Fat 0g	0%
Sodium 27mg	1%
Total Carbohydrate 38g	11%
Sugars 38g	
Protein 0g	

* Percent Daily Values are based on a 2,000 calorie diet.

INGREDIENTS: CARBONATED WATER, PURE CANE SUGAR, CARAMEL COLOR, SODIUM BENZOATE (A PRESERVATIVE) CITRIC ACID, NATURAL FLAVOR.

WWW.DEADWORLDZOMBIESODA.COM

8 57428 00508 3

Label #46

Bottled by Intrastate Distributors Inc, 20021 Exeter St, Detroit, MI 48203

CA CASH REFUND . CT . MA . VT . NY . ME . IA . OR .
HI 5¢ REFUND . MI 10¢ REFUND

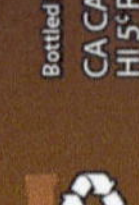
Please Recycle

MAHTROX's

SOUR APPLE SLUDGE

TWIZTID

POWERED BY DEADWORLD

Caprice Brands and DeadWorld Beverages are trademarks of Caprice Brands, LLC. DeadWorld is a trademark and copyright of Gary Reed and used with permission. All rights reserved.

Caprice

Nutrition Facts

Serving Size 1 Can (325.0 g)

Amount Per Serving

Calories 180	Calories from Fat 54
	% Daily Value*
Total Fat 6.0g	9%
Saturated Fat 2.5g	12%
Polyunsaturated Fat 0.5g	
Monounsaturated Fat 2.5g	
Cholesterol 5mg	2%
Sodium 200mg	8%
Total Carbohydrates 24.0g	8%
Dietary Fiber 5.0g	20%
Sugars 17.0g	
Protein 10.0g	
Vitamin A 35% •	Vitamin C 100%
Calcium 50% •	Iron 15%

* Based on a 2000 calorie diet

INGREDIENTS: CARBONATED WATER, INVERT CANE SUGAR, NATURAL FLAVOURS, CITRIC ACID, SODIUM BENZOATE, CARAMEL, POTASSIUM SORBATE.

0 36000 29145 2

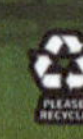
PLEASE RECYCLE

Bottled by Intrastate Distributors Inc, 20021 Exeter St, Detroit, MI 48203

CA CASH REFUND . CT . MA . VT . NY . ME . IA . OR .
HI 5¢ REFUND . MI . 10¢ REFUND

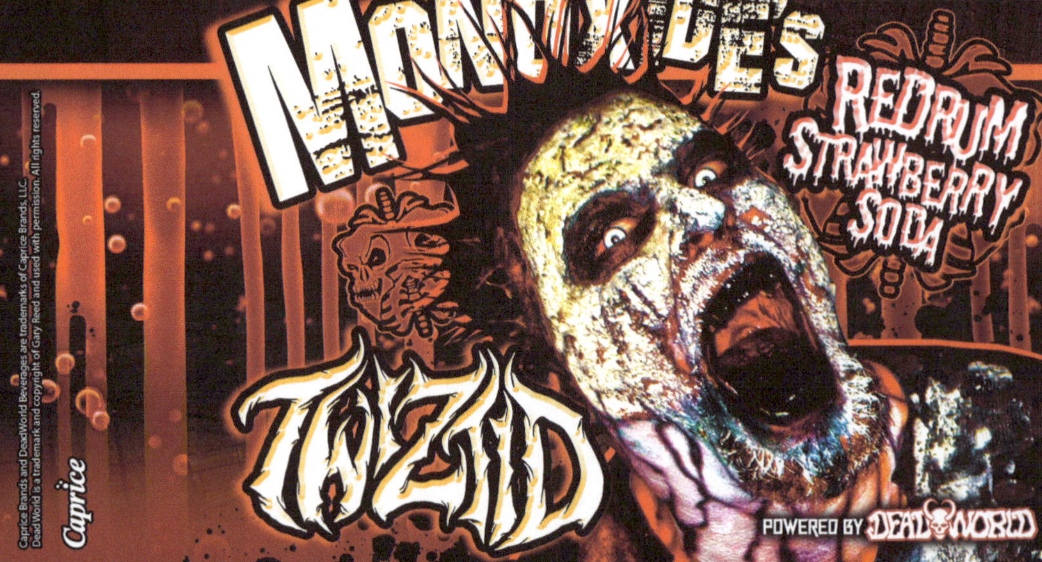

REDRUM STRAWBERRY SODA

POWERED BY DEADWORLD

Caprice Brands and DeadWorld Beverages are trademarks of Caprice Brands, LLC. DeadWorld is a trademark and copyright of Gary Reed and used with permission. All rights reserved.

Caprice

Nutrition Facts

Serving Size 1 Can (325.0 g)

Amount Per Serving

Calories 180	Calories from Fat 54
	% Daily Value*
Total Fat 6.0g	9%
Saturated Fat 2.5g	12%
Polyunsaturated Fat 0.5g	
Monounsaturated Fat 2.5g	
Cholesterol 5mg	2%
Sodium 200mg	8%
Total Carbohydrates 24.0g	8%
Dietary Fiber 5.0g	20%
Sugars 17.0g	
Protein 10.0g	
Vitamin A 35% •	Vitamin C 100%
Calcium 50% •	Iron 15%

* Based on a 2000 calorie diet

INGREDIENTS: CARBONATED WATER, INVERT CANE SUGAR, NATURAL FLAVOURS, CITRIC ACID, SODIUM BENZOATE, CARAMEL, POTASSIUM SORBATE.

0 36000 29145 2

PLEASE RECYCLE

Bottled by Intrastate Distributors Inc, 20021 Exeter St, Detroit, MI 48203

CA CASH REFUND . CT . MA . VT . NY . ME . IA . OR .
HI 5¢ REFUND . MI . 10¢ REFUND

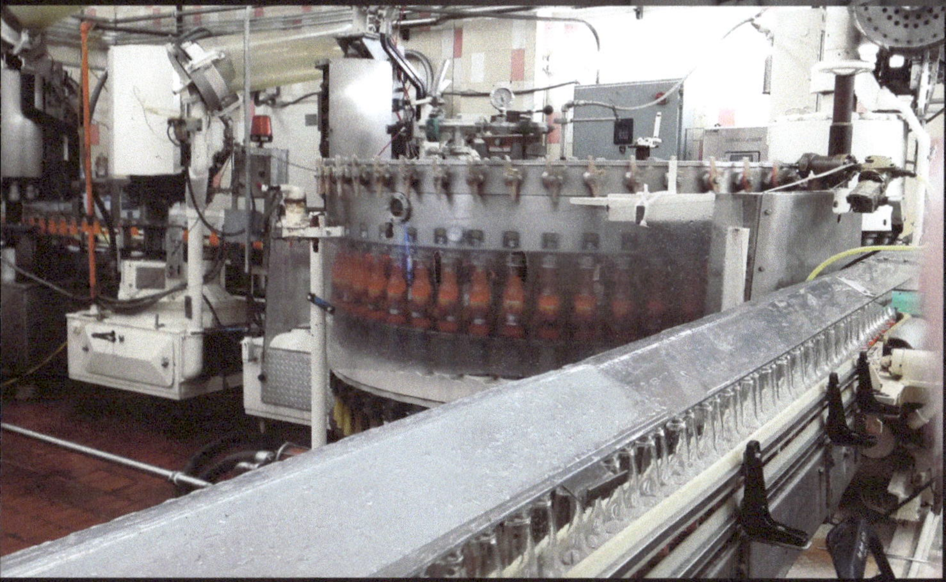

PRODUCTION

The bottles being filled by the machines in the bottling plant.

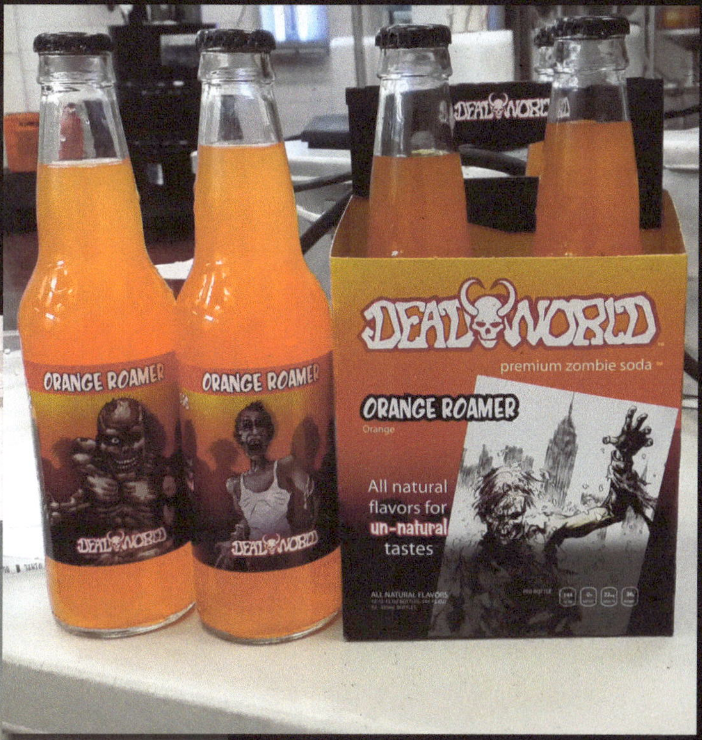

The first case of soda off the line!

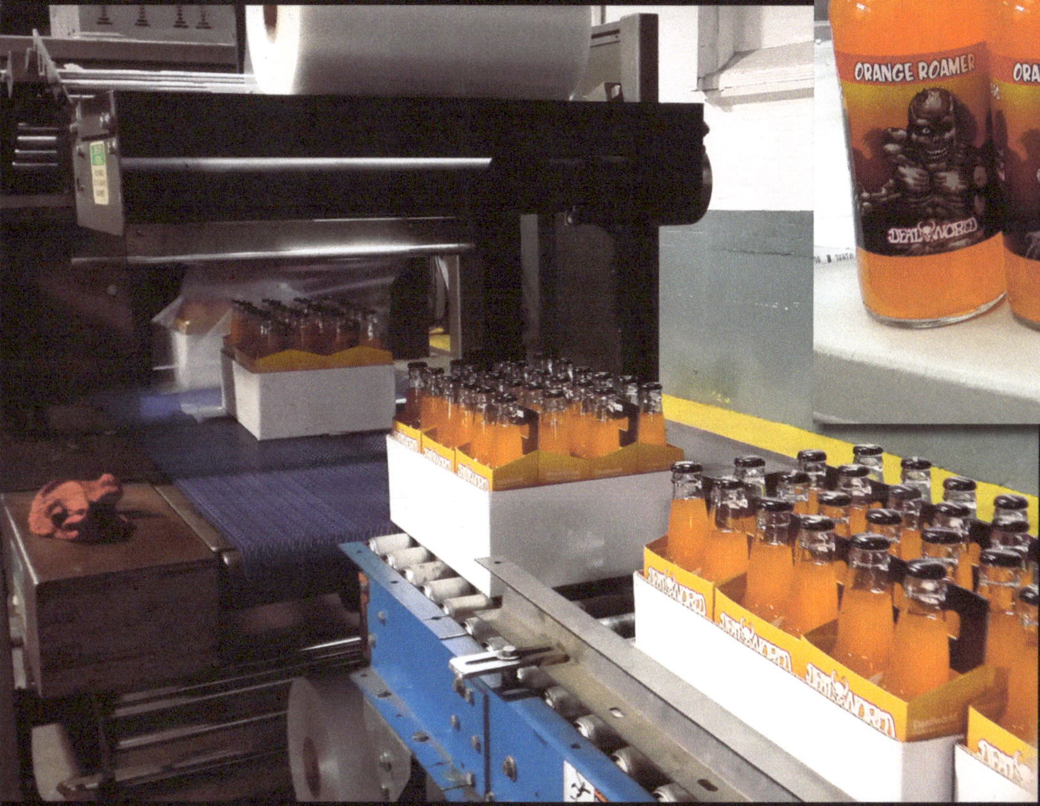

The first cases of Deadworld being shrinkwrapped.

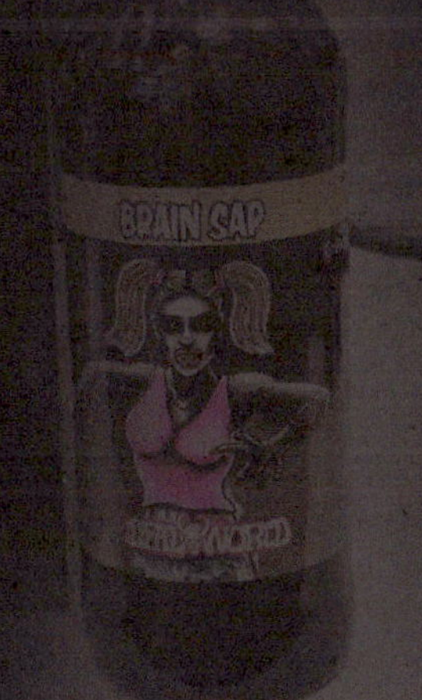

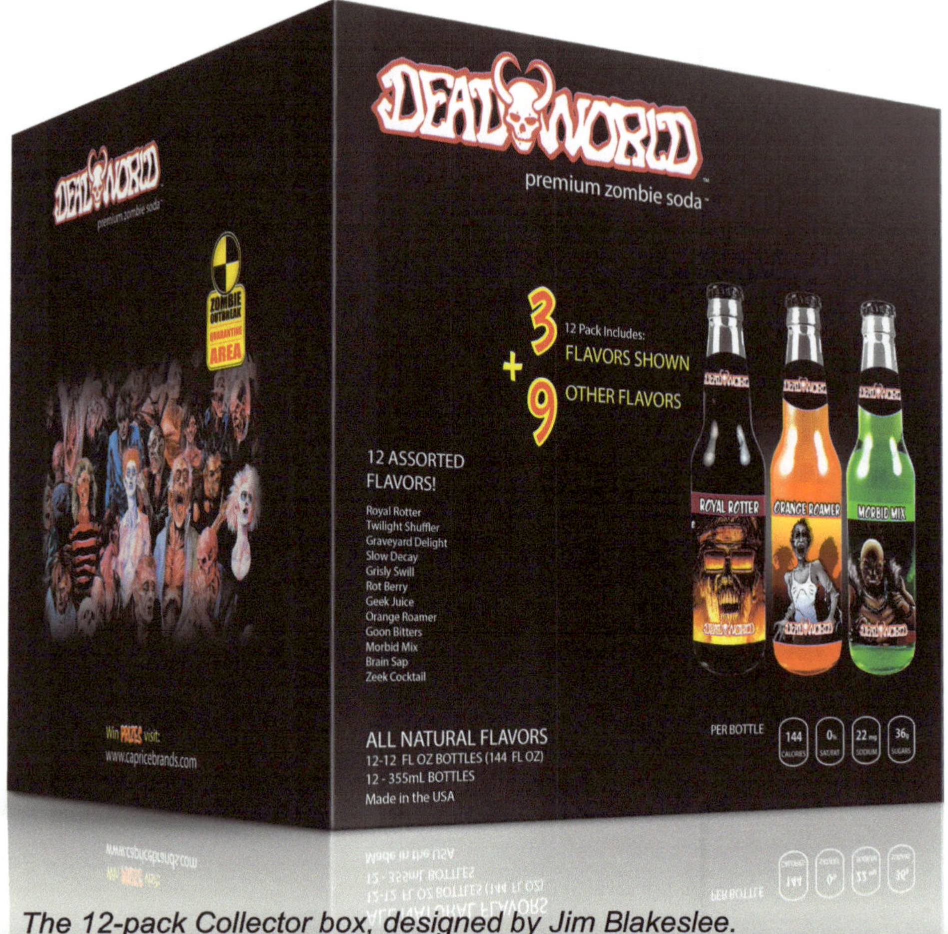

The 12-pack Collector box, designed by Jim Blakeslee.

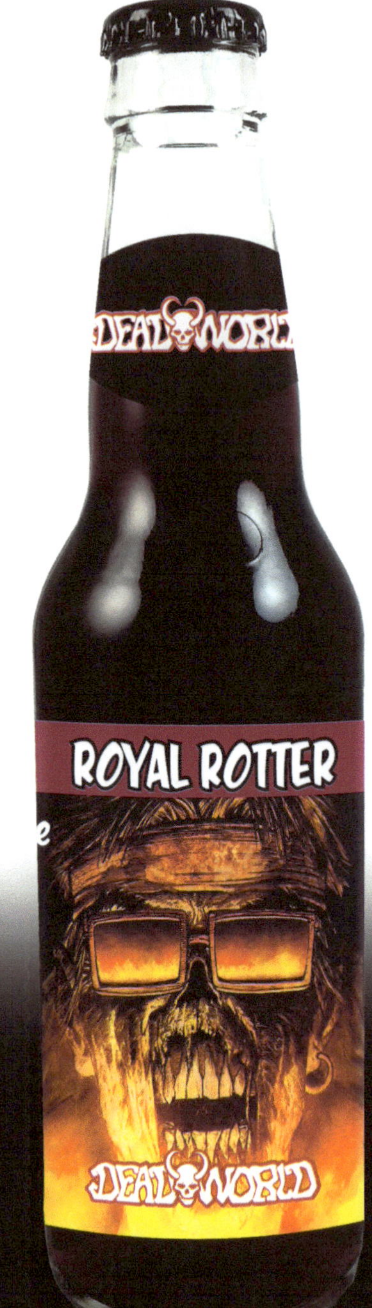

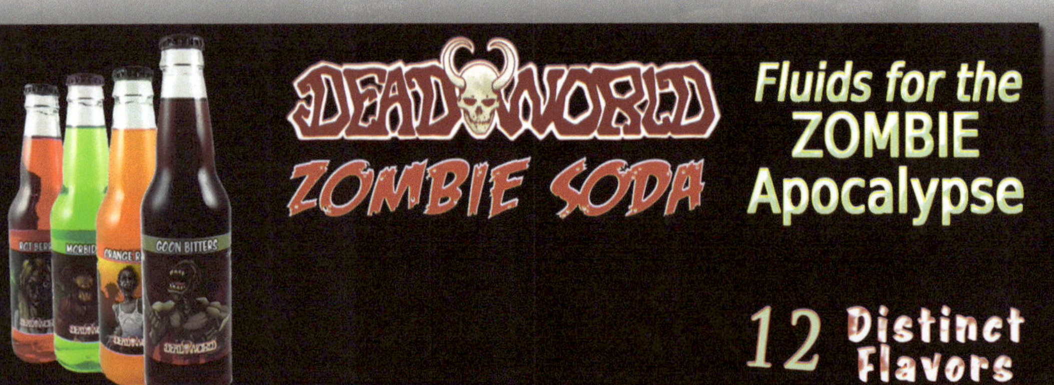

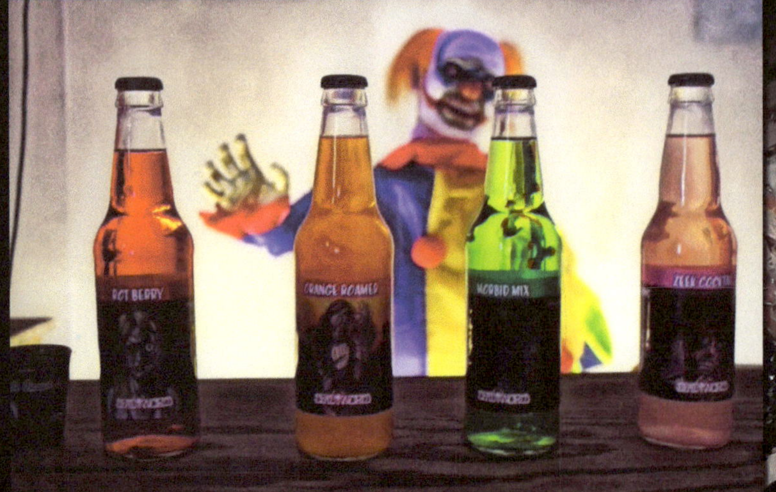

Promotional photo by Bonnie Brown.

ZOMBIE QUARANTINE

DEADWORLD ZOMBIE SODA INTRODUCTION EVENT

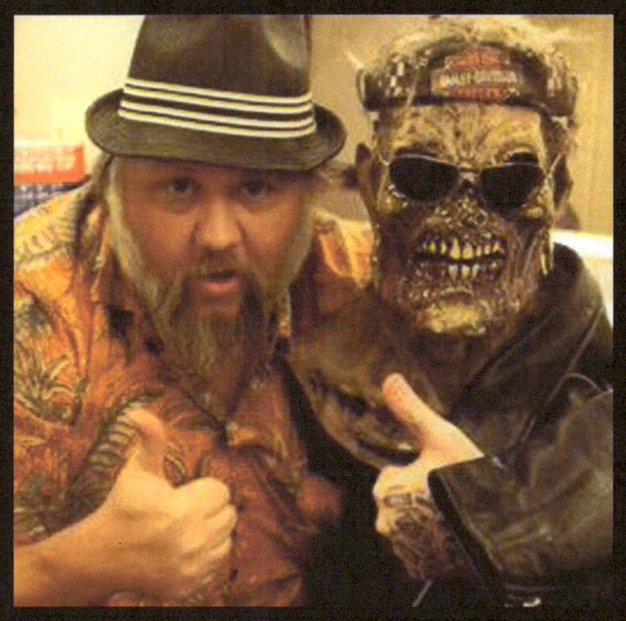

Dennis Barger with King Zombie. (Dennis is on the left).

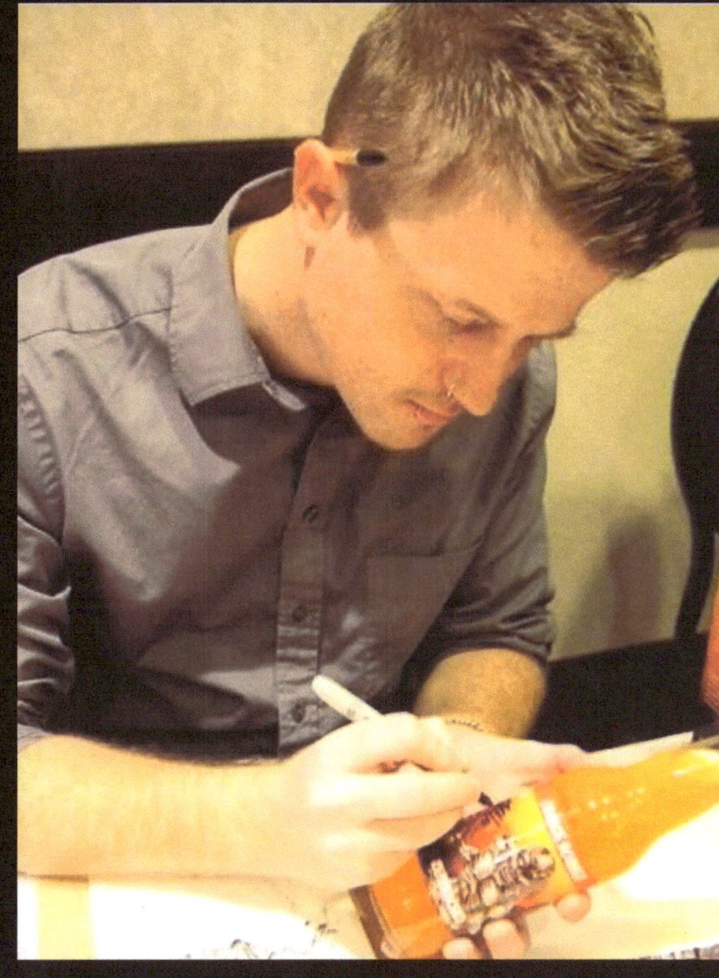

Artist Joshua Werner autographing a bottle.

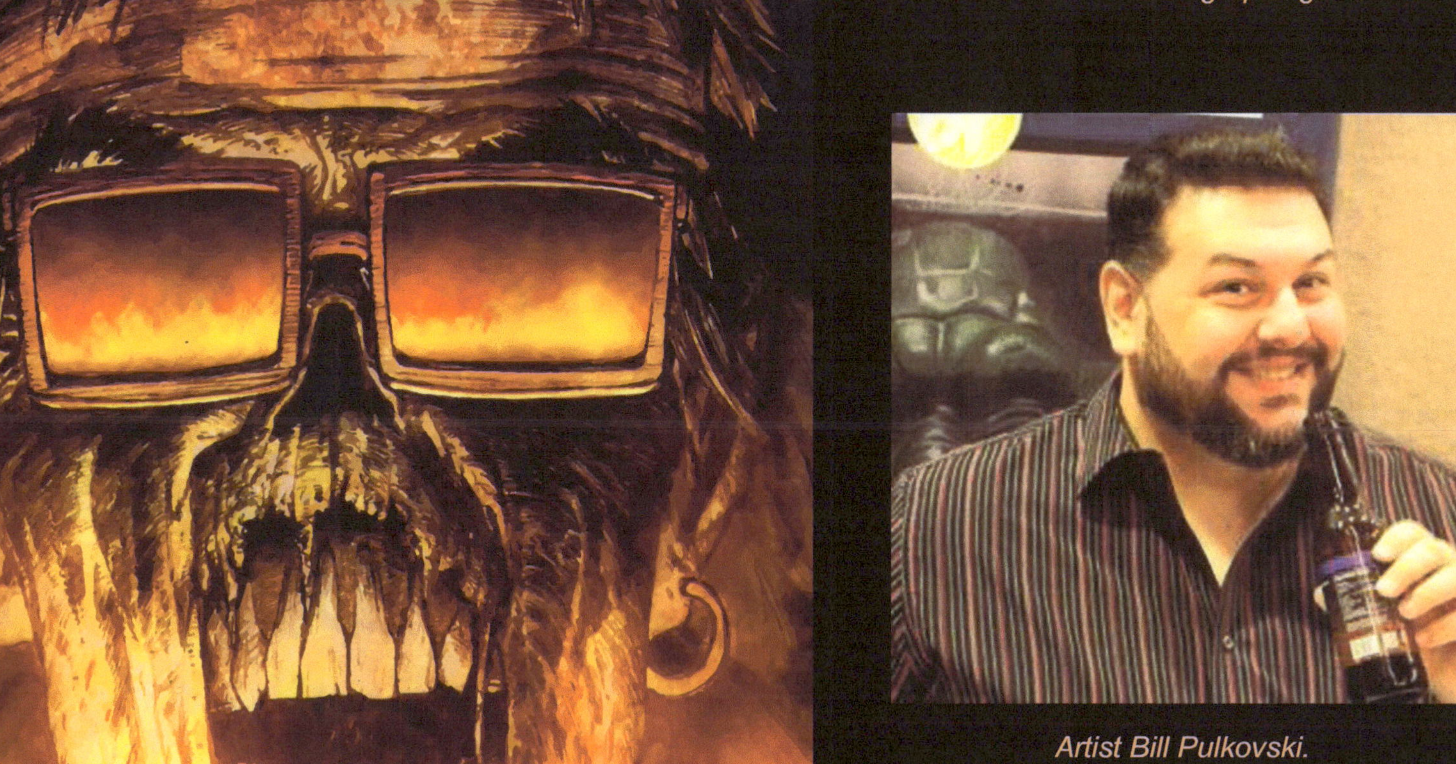

Artist Bill Pulkovski.

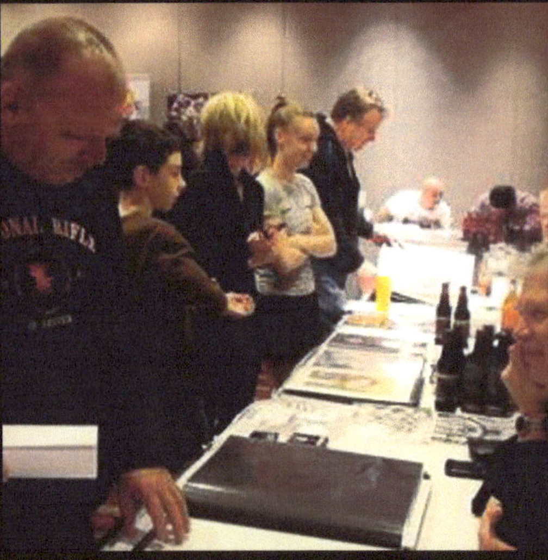

Fans meeting the artists.

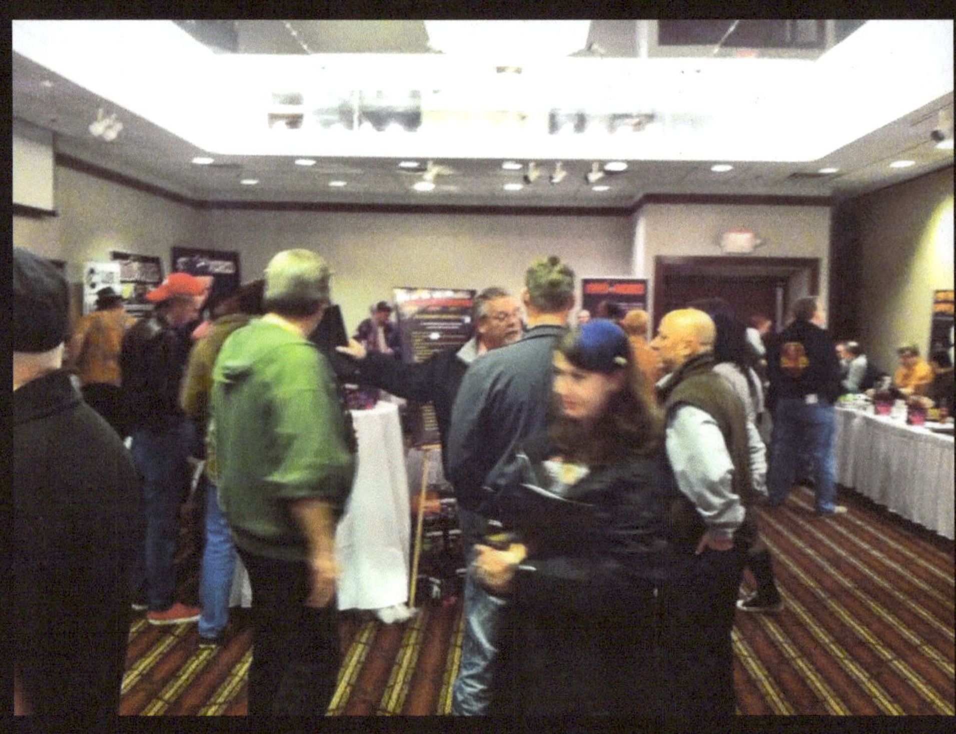

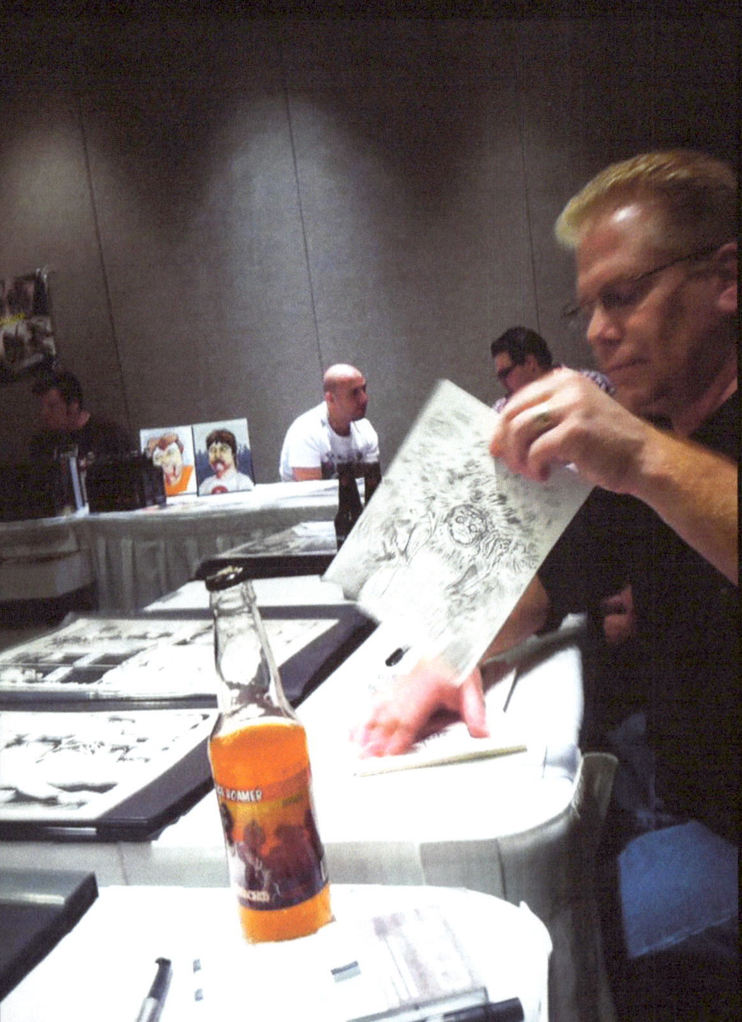

Artist Mark Bloodworth finishing a drawing.

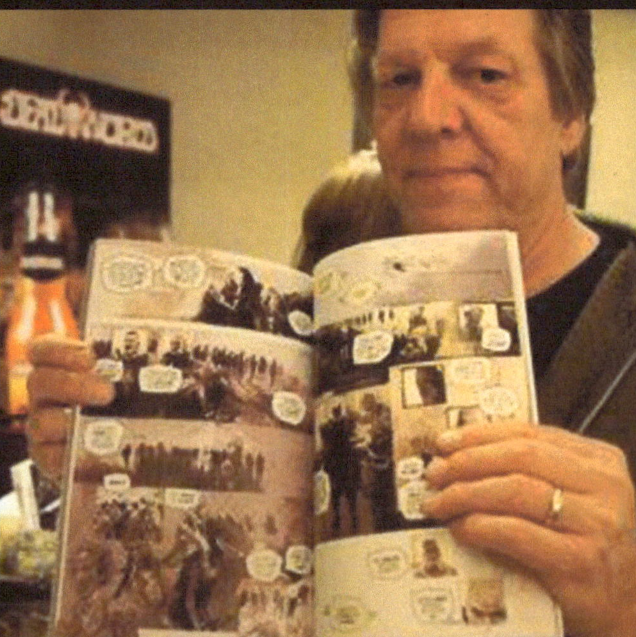

Gary Reed with a Deadworld comic at the event.

ZOMBIE QUARANTINE

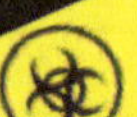

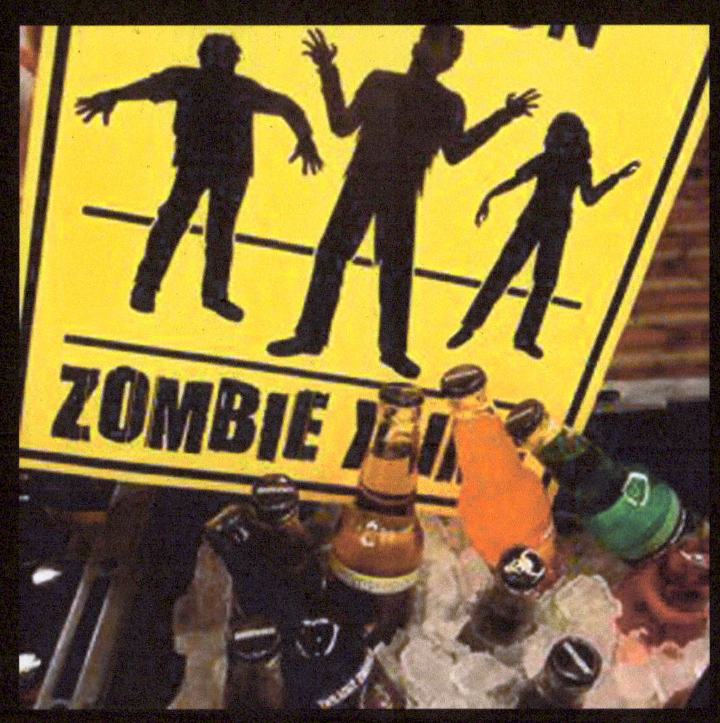

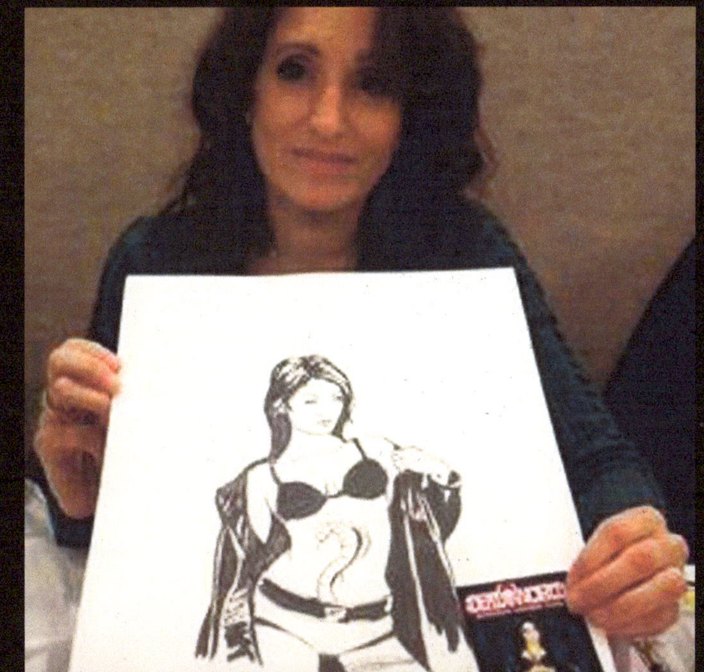

Artist Anne Garavaglia with one of her drawings.

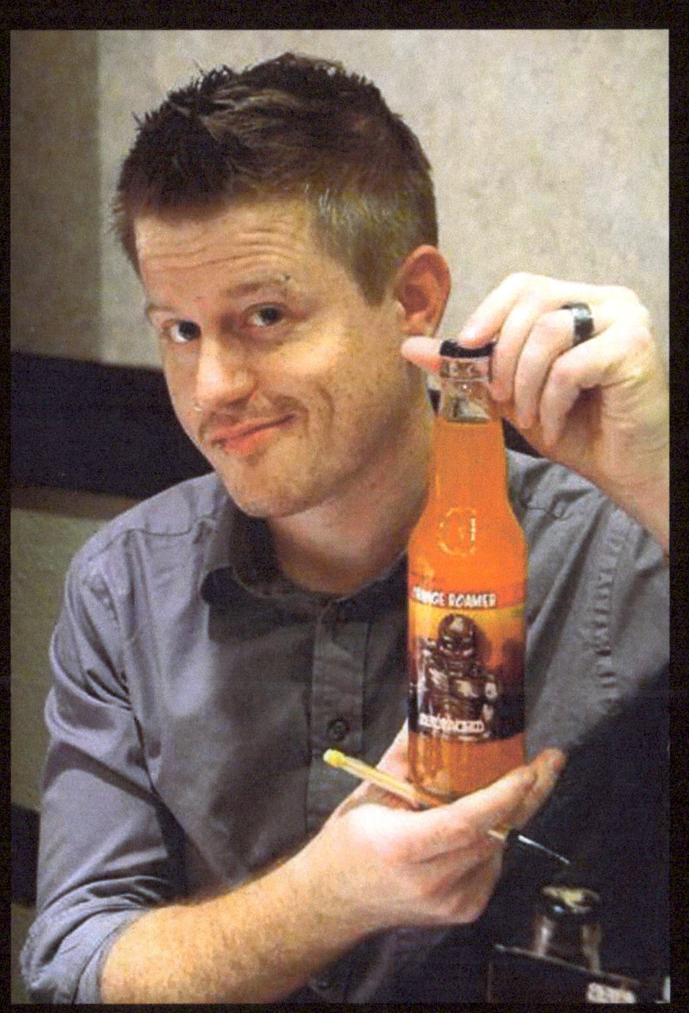

Joshua Werner with a bottle of Orange Roamer.

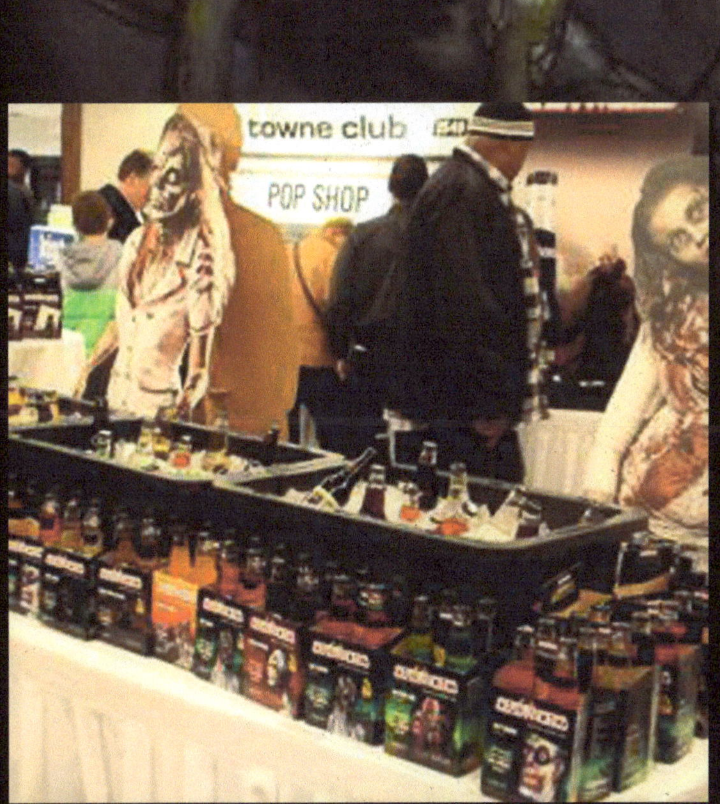

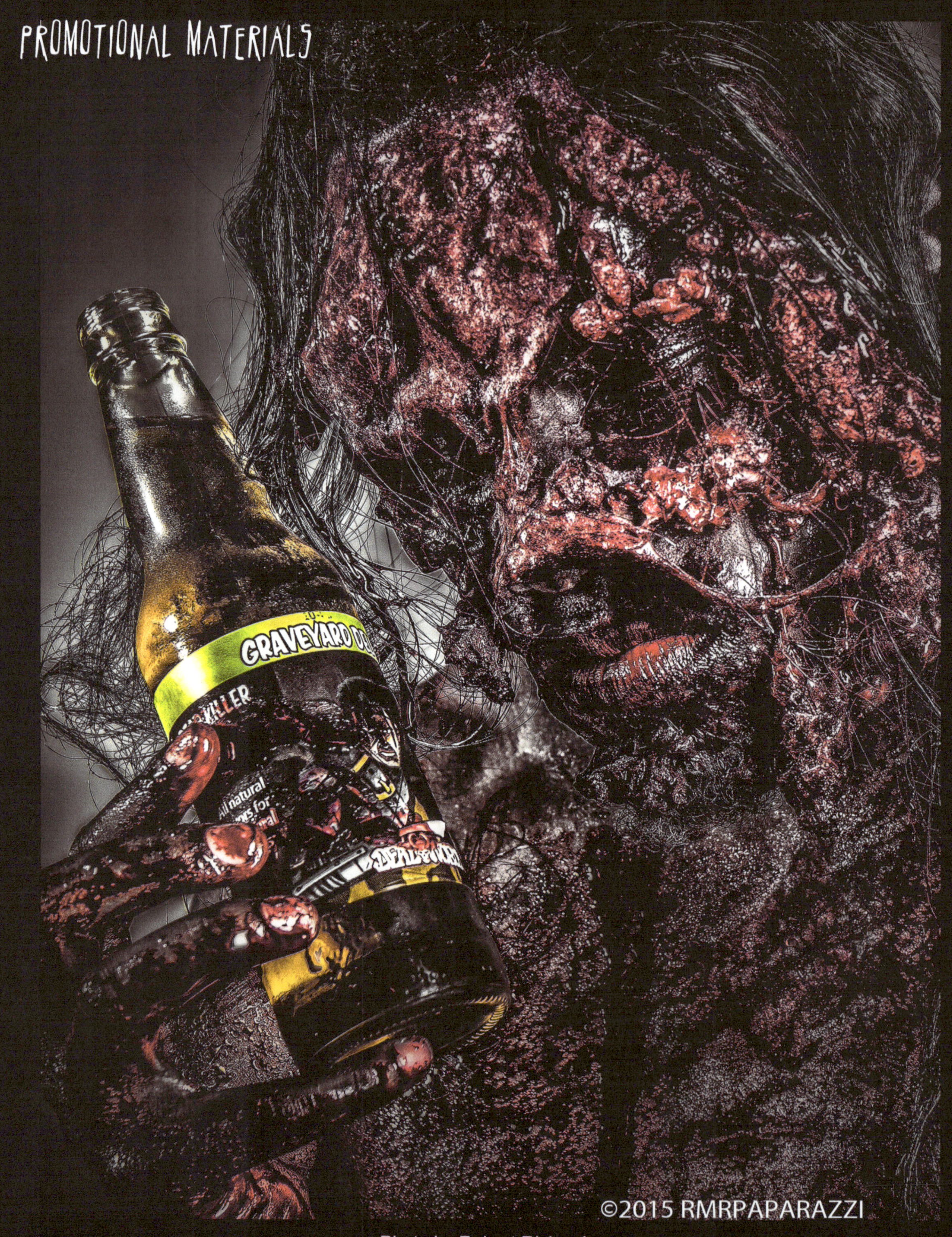

Photo by Robert Richards.

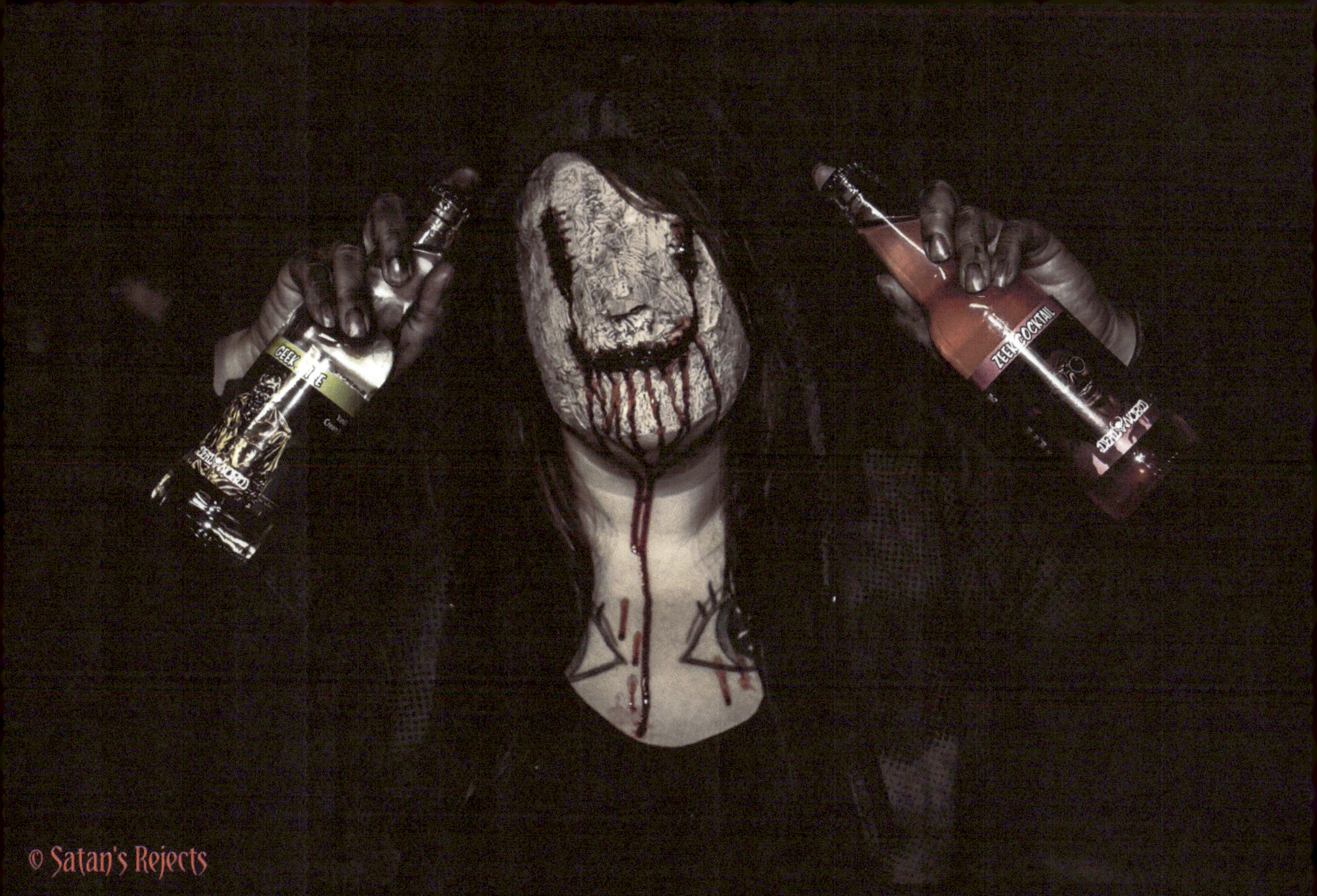

© Satan's Rejects

Above: Bailey Ledford. Photo by Steve Savage Smith.
Below: Custom car builder Carol Moraca. Photo by Steve Moraca.

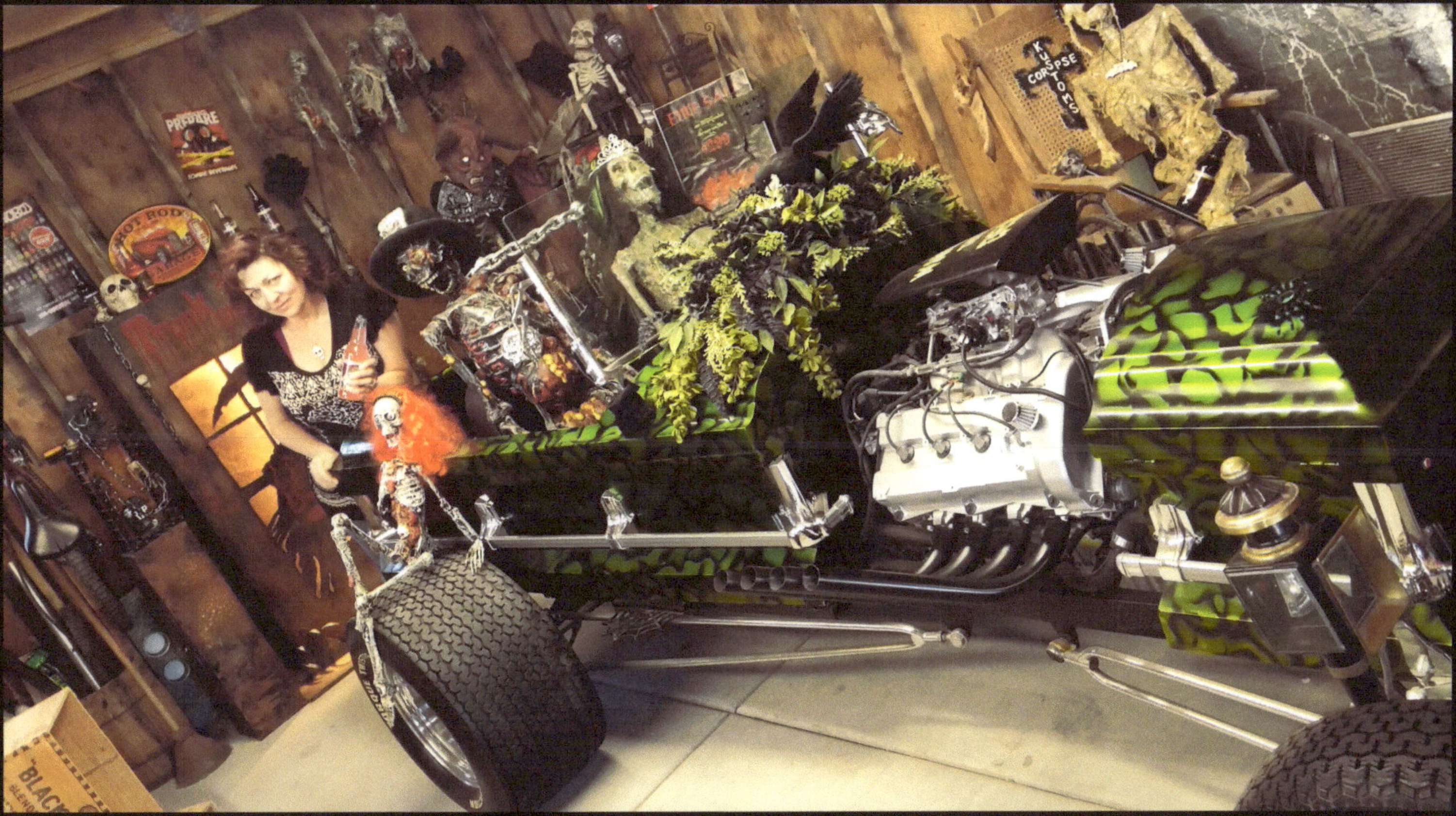

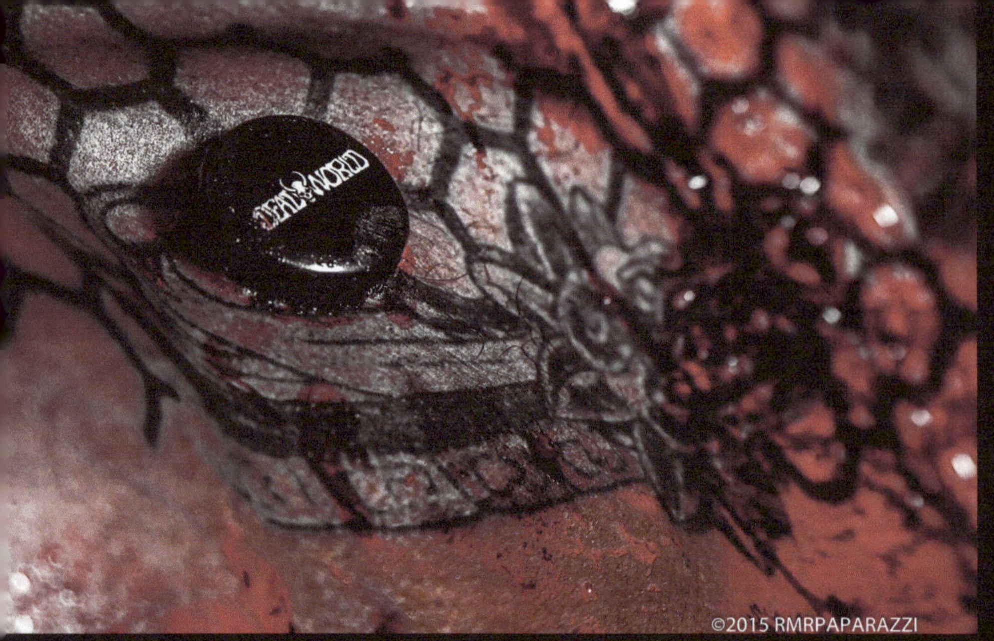

Above: Photo by Robert Richards.
Below: Janelle Powers with Twiztid.

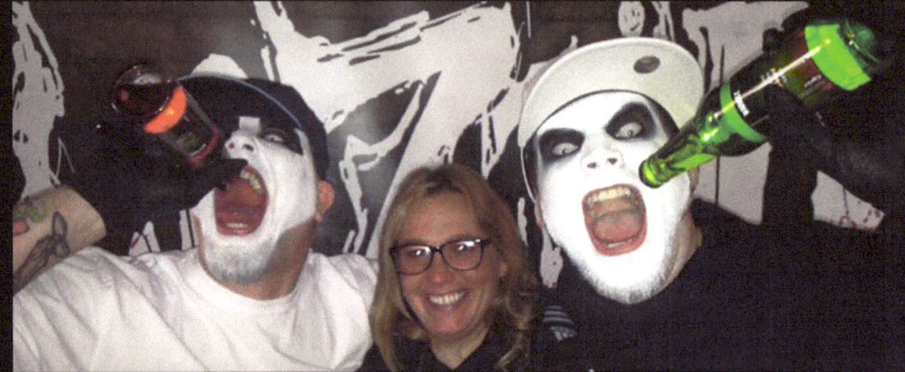

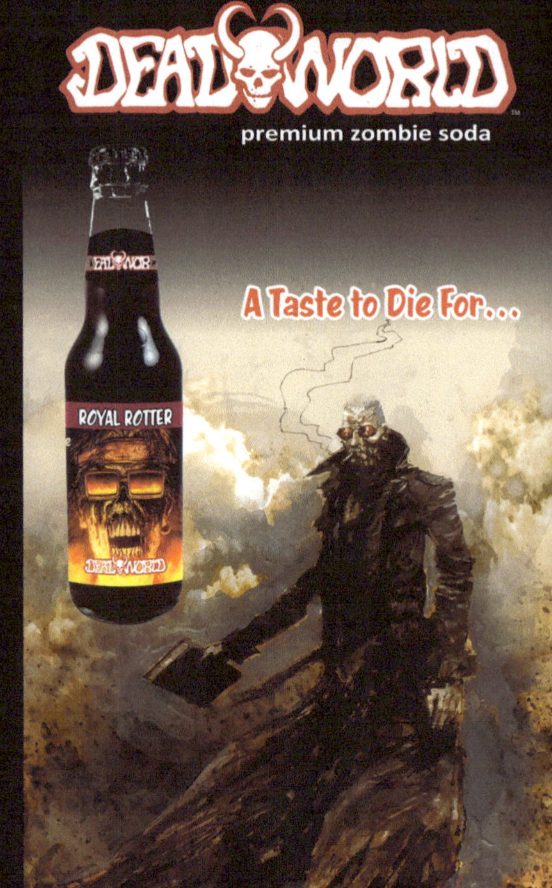

Below: Photo by Robert Richards.

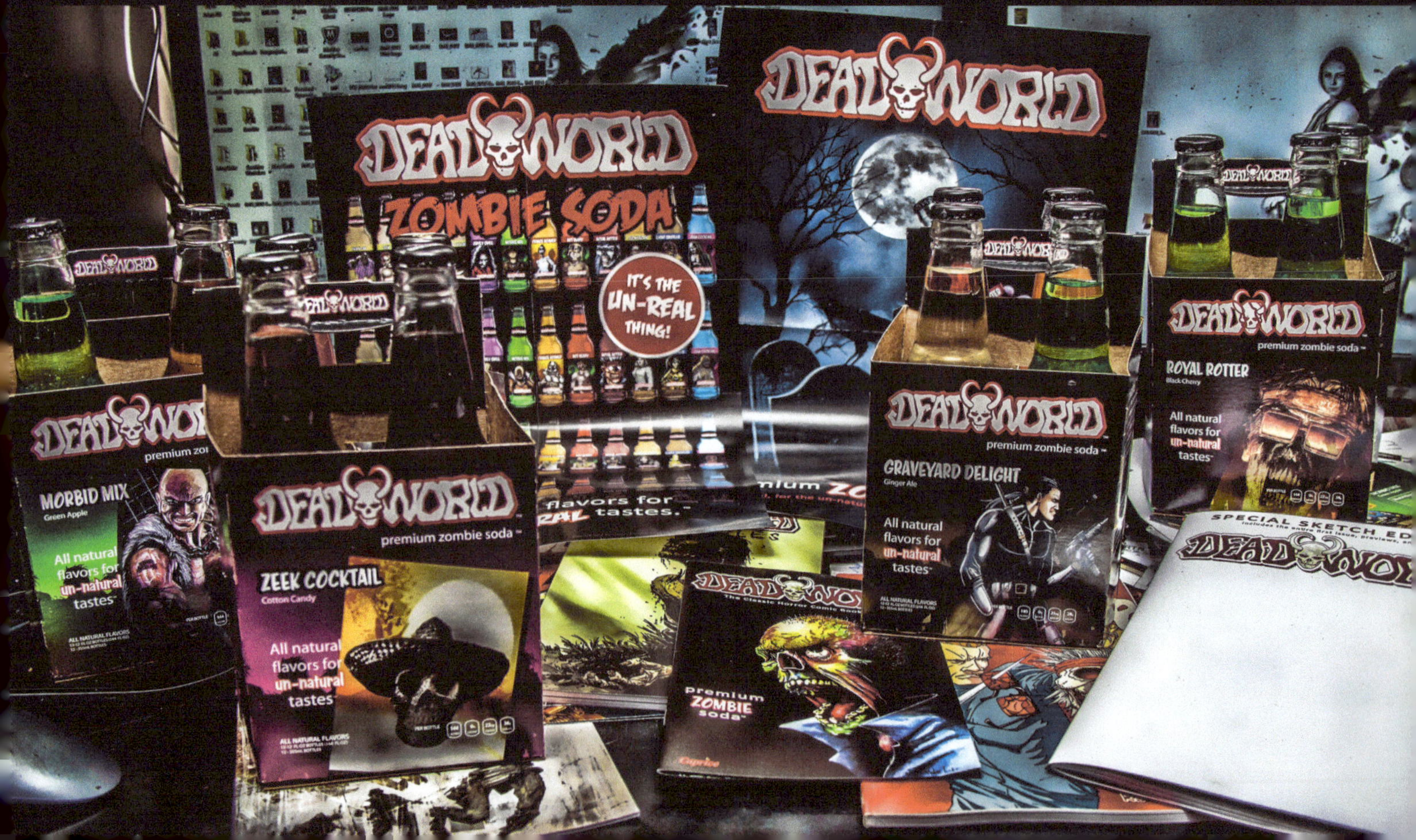

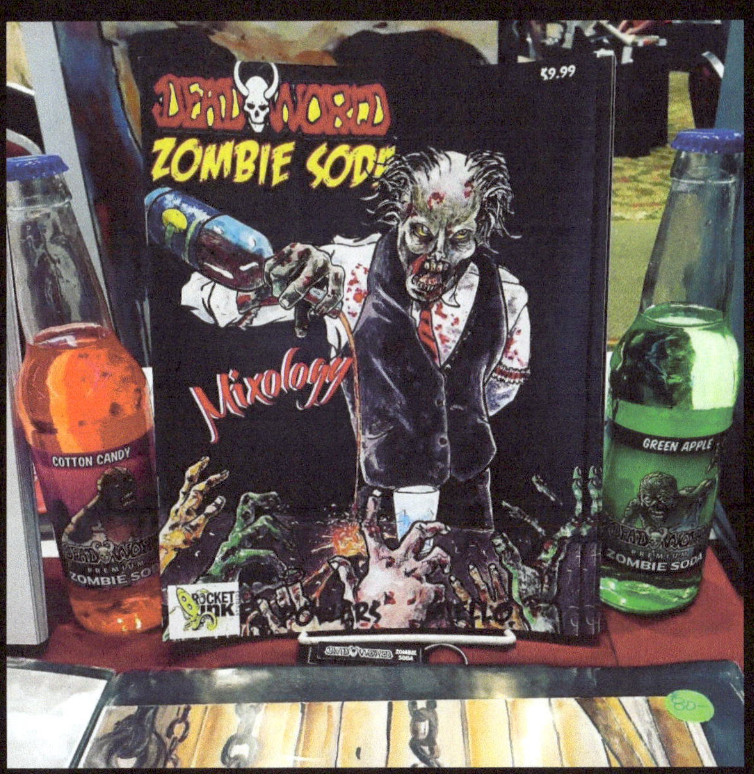

Deadworld Zombie Soda Mixology book by Tony Miello and Janelle Powers.

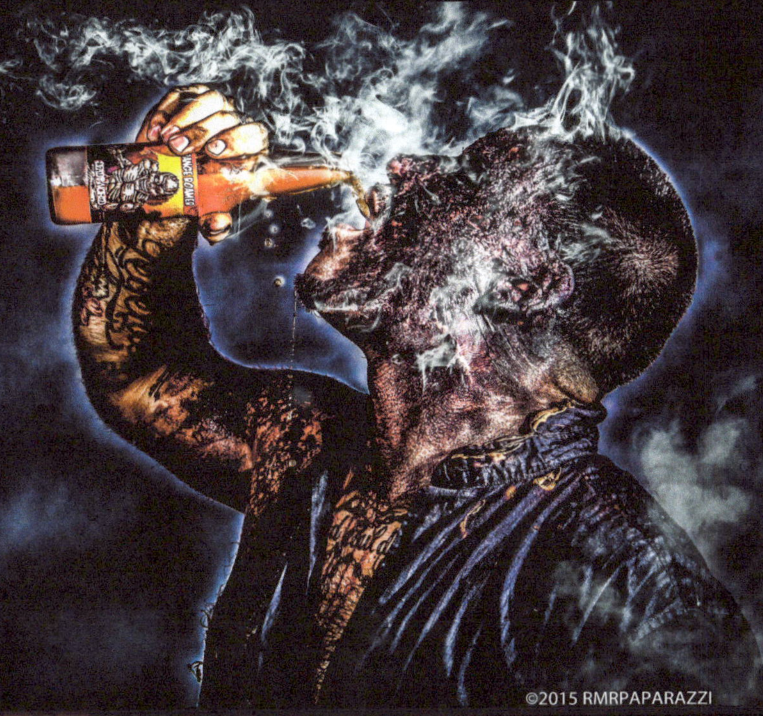

Photo by Robert Richards.

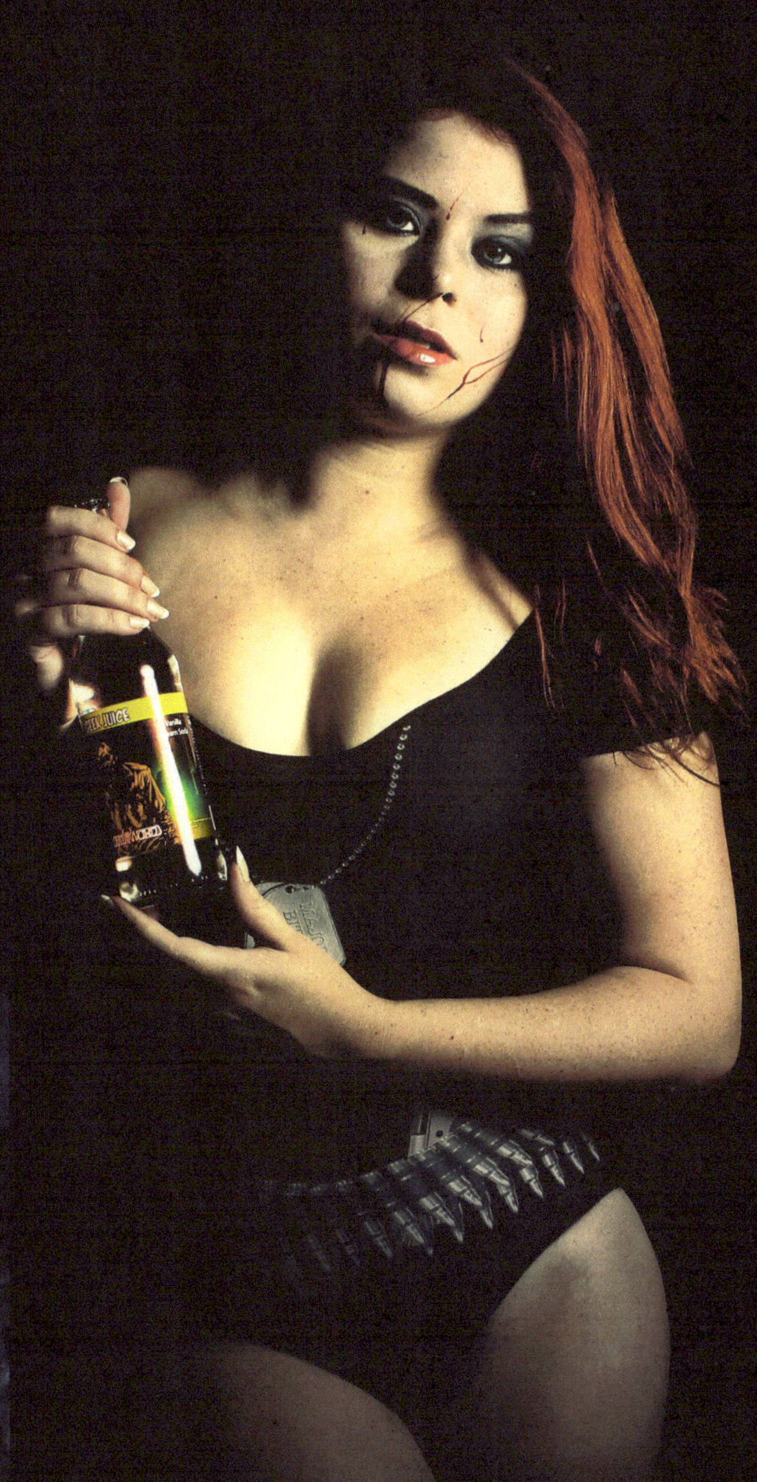

Photo by Mel Heflin.

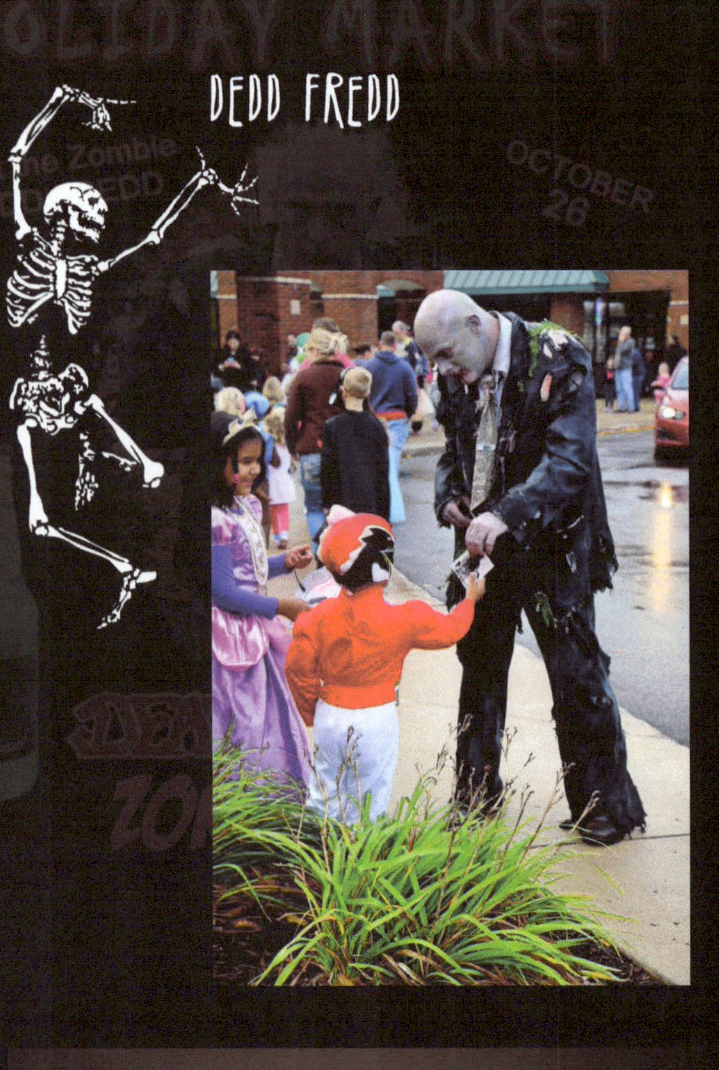

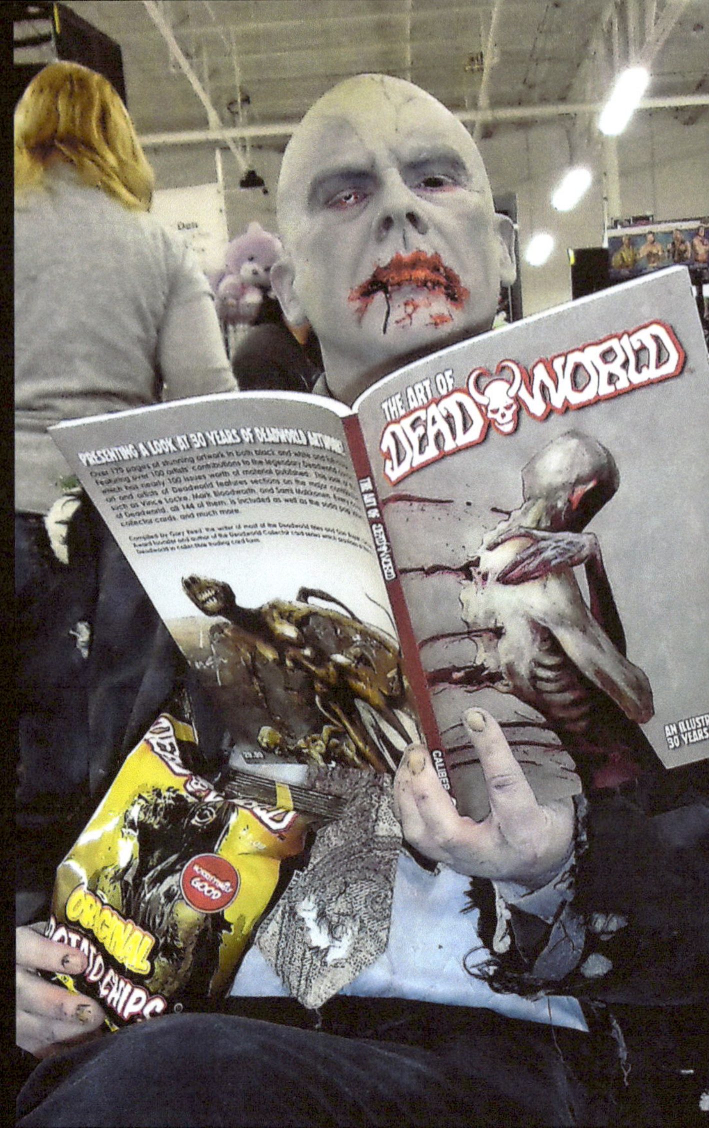

Photo by Chelsea Kennedy.

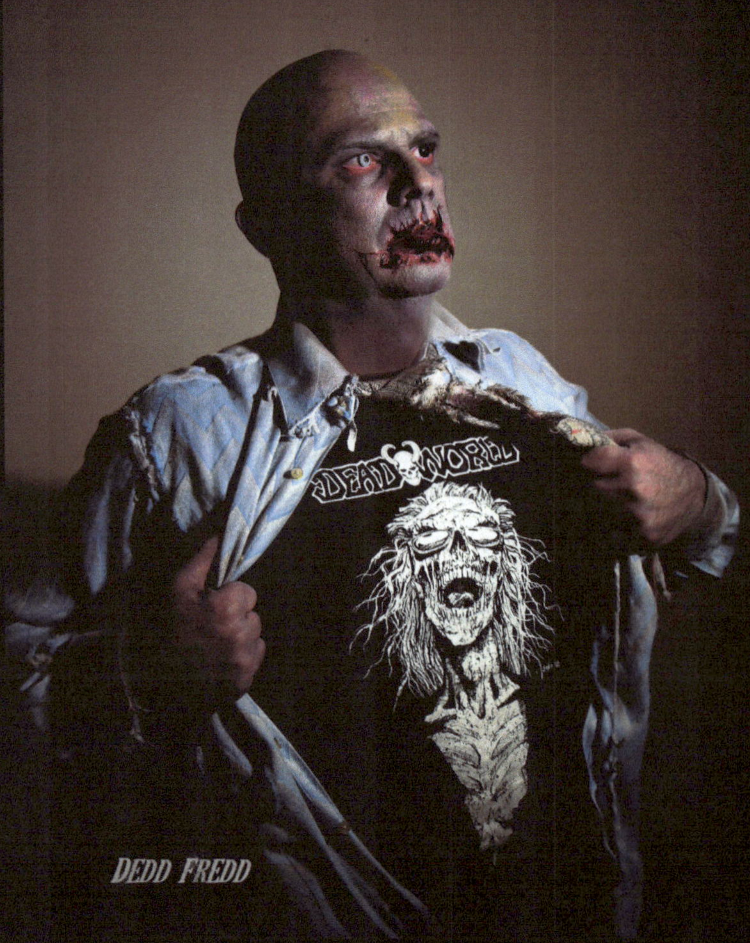

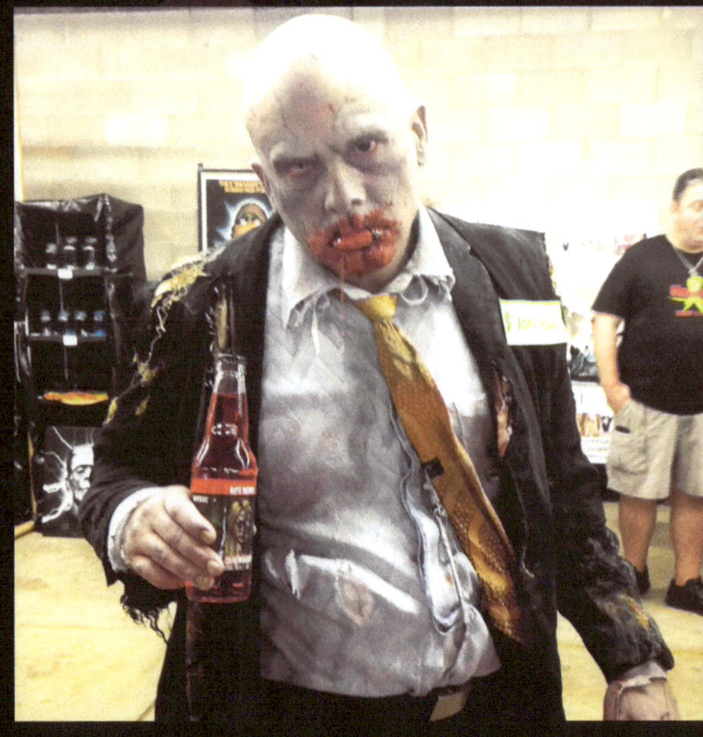

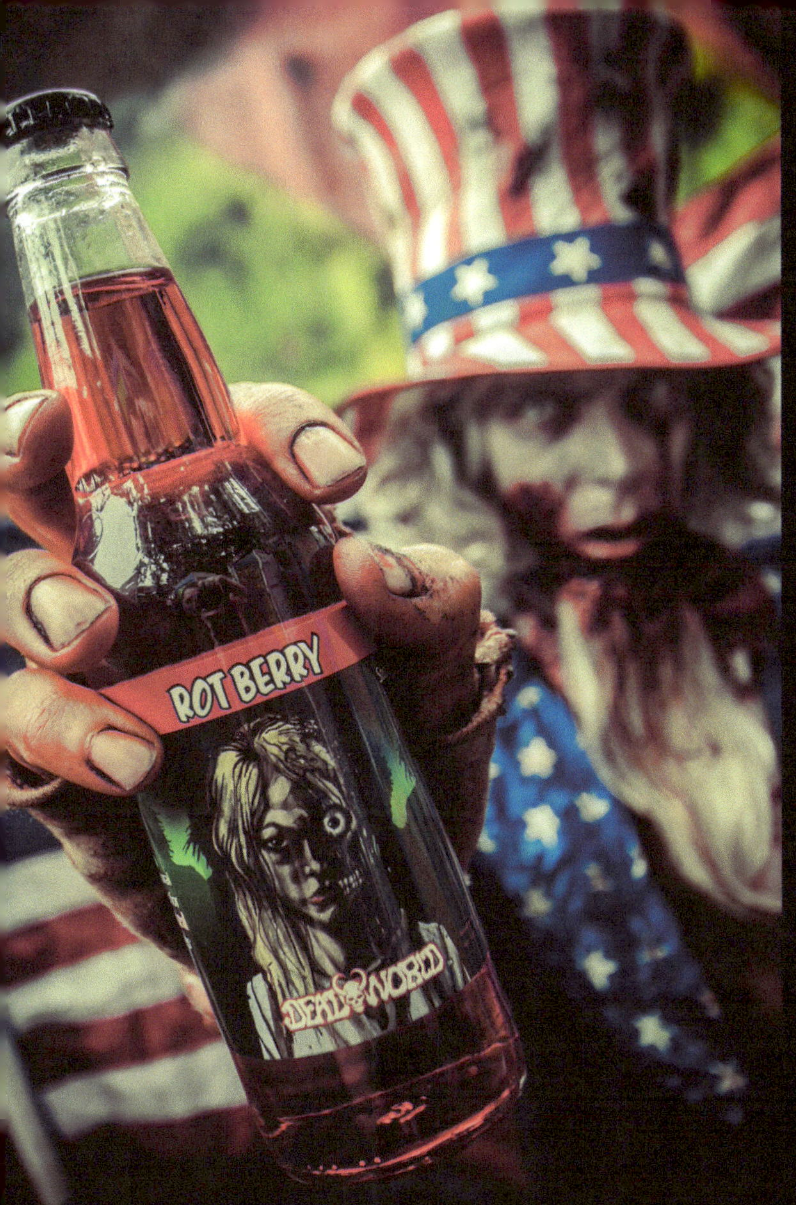

Above: Uncle Zombie Jeff, photo by Jeff Beach.
Below: Delivery Zombie Jeff, photo by Janelle Powers.

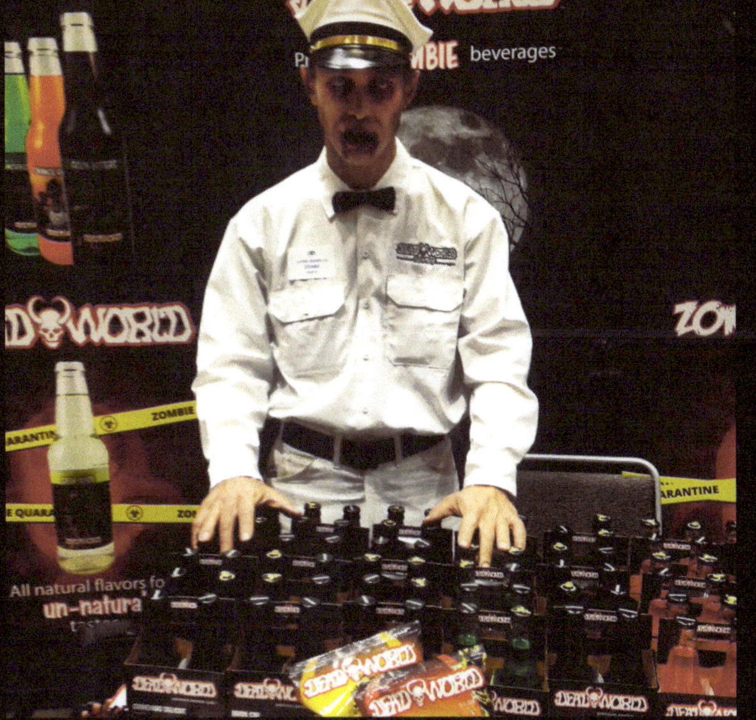

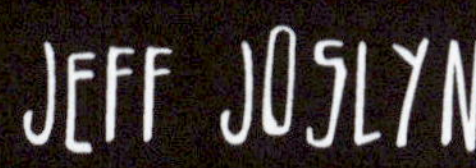

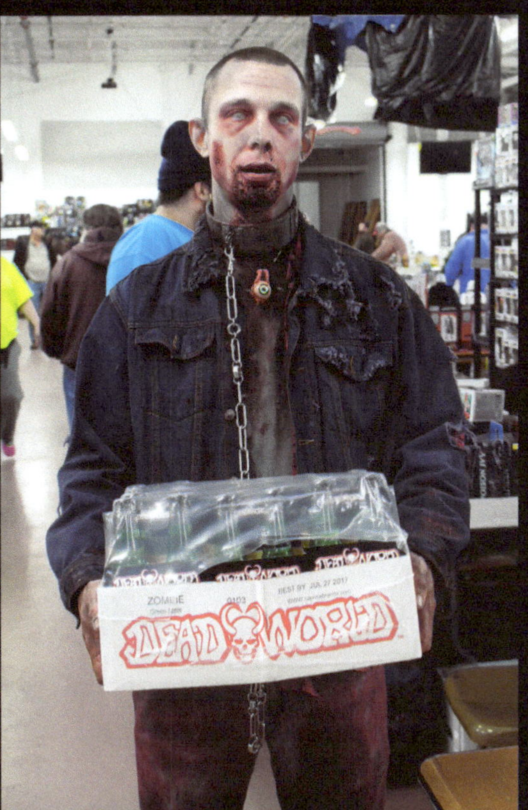

Above: Photo by Bonnie Brown.
Below: Photo by Jeff Beach.

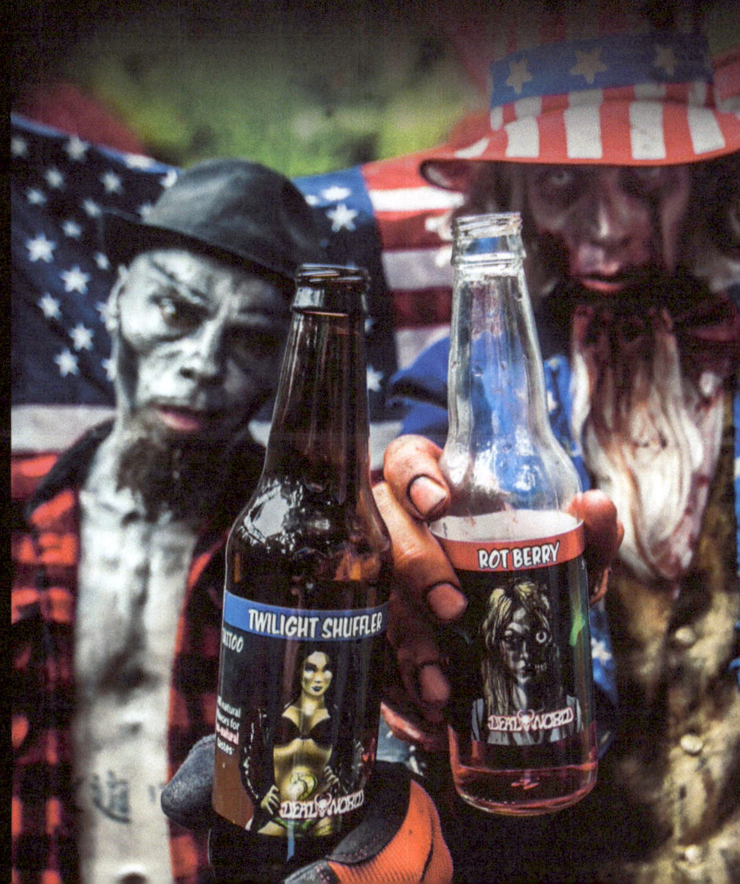

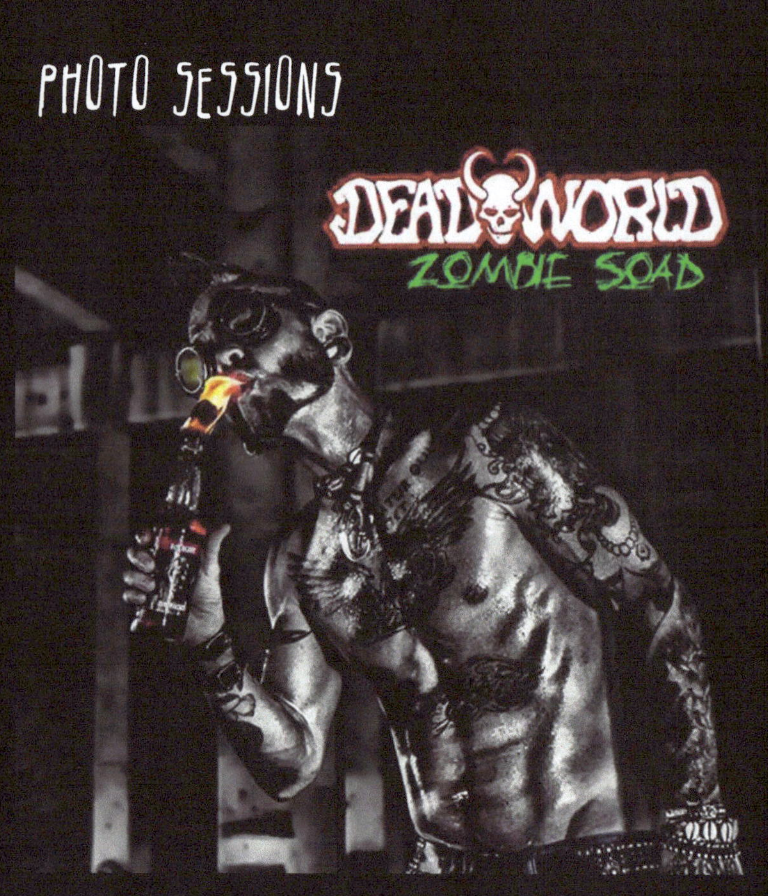

Above: Charley Hayes, photo by Robert Richards.
Below: Candy Carnage, photo by Eric Littlefield

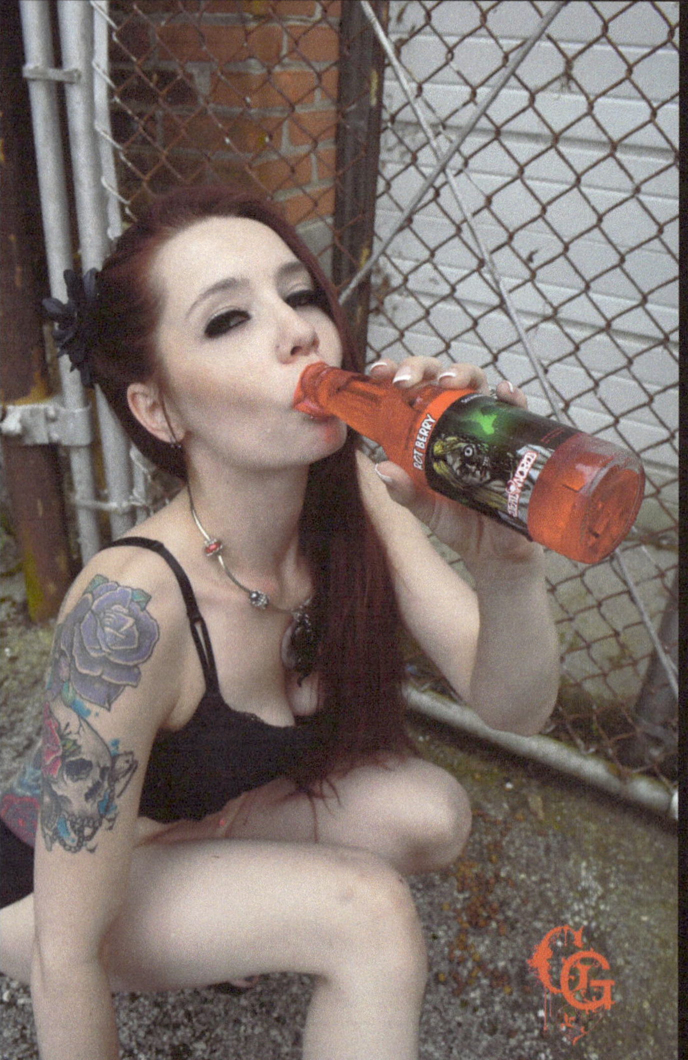

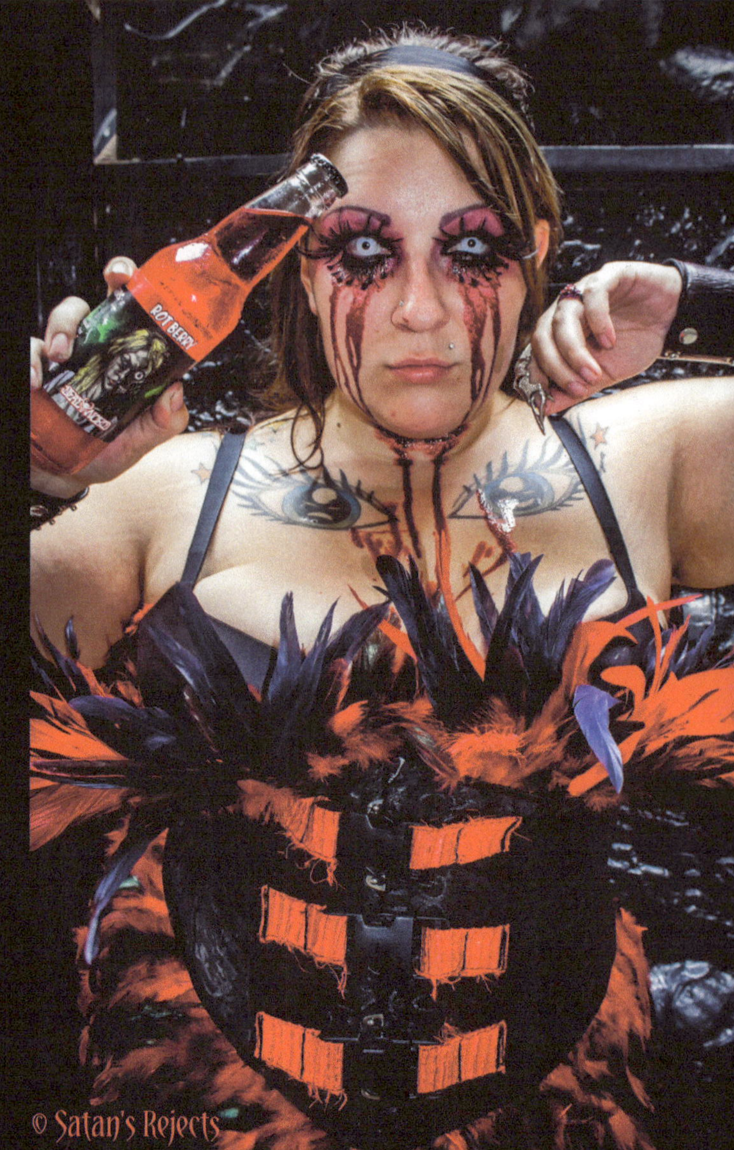

Bailey Marie, photo by Steve Savage Smith.

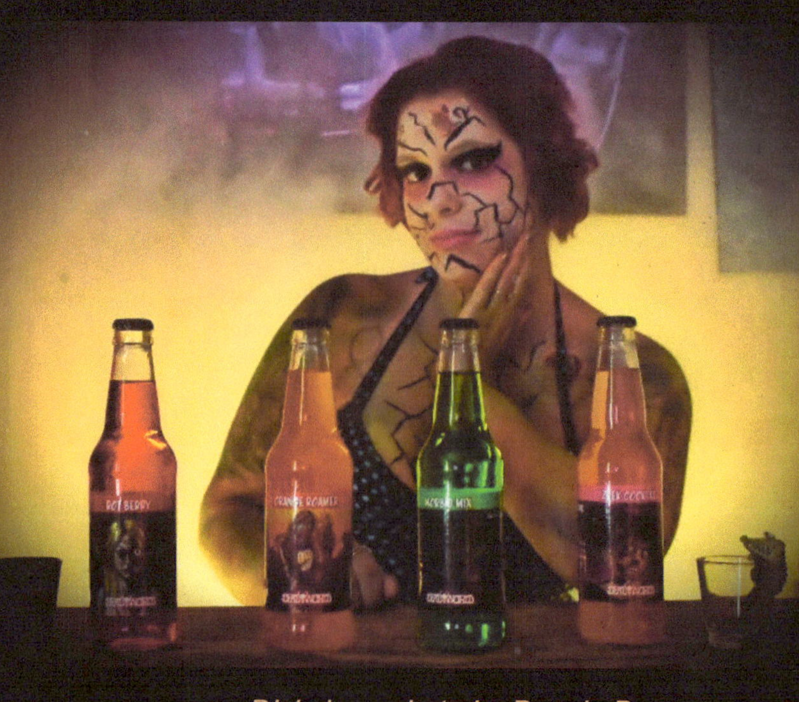

Dixie Lee, photo by Bonnie Brown.

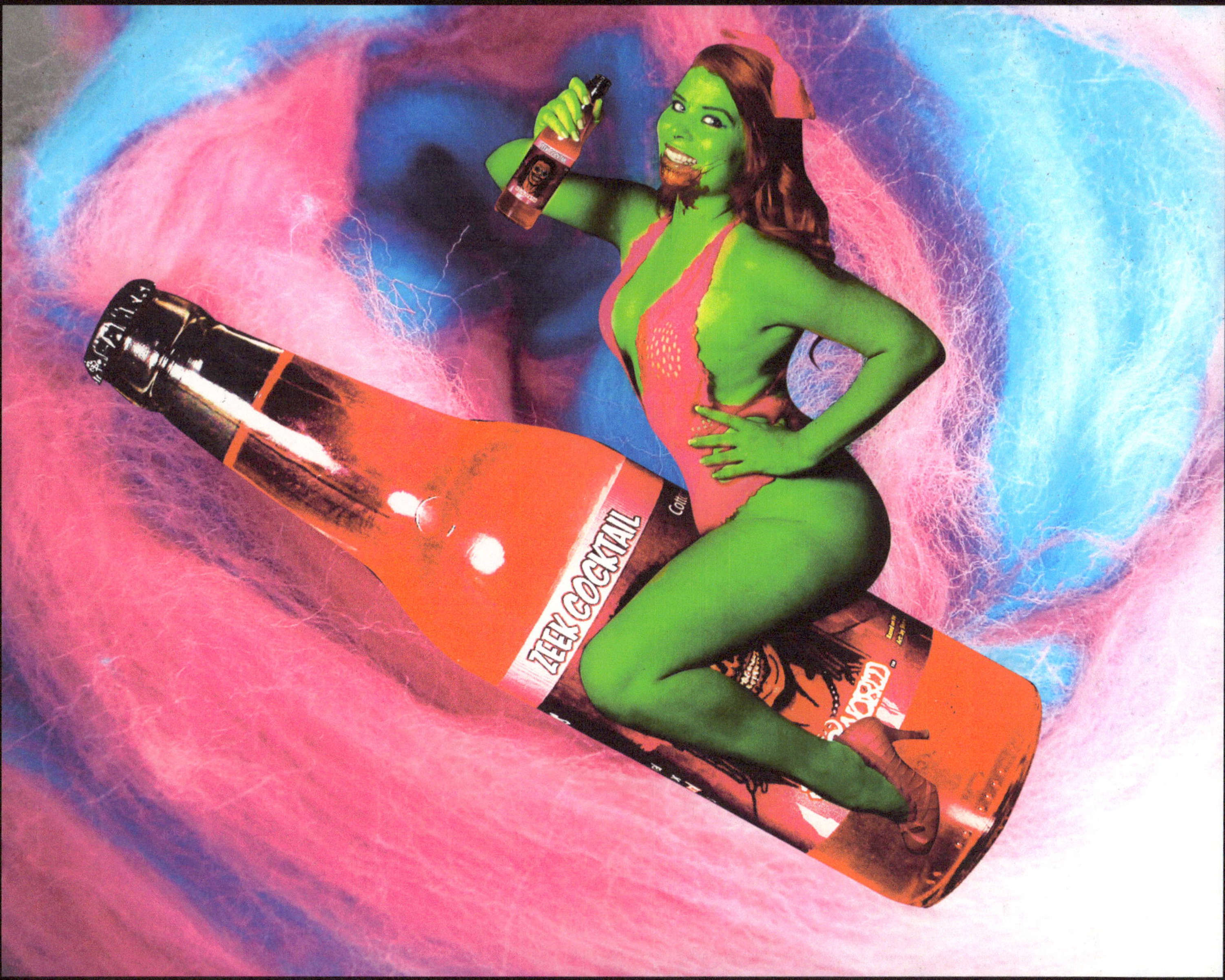

Cotton Candy Zombie, photo by Mel Heflin.

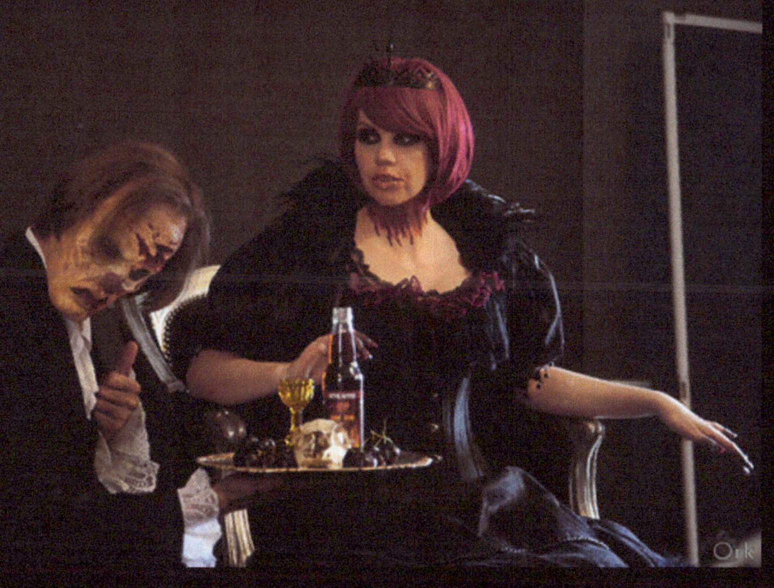

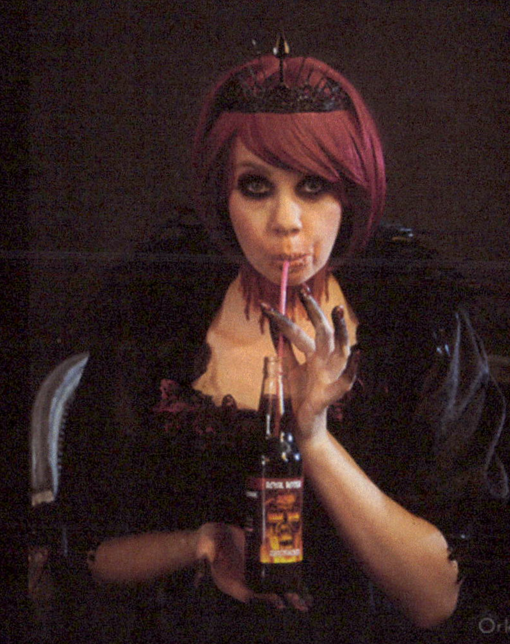

Above: Dick Carlier and Catherine Moon at the Netherlands Photo Shoot. Photo by Darkashter. Right: Photo by Darkashter.

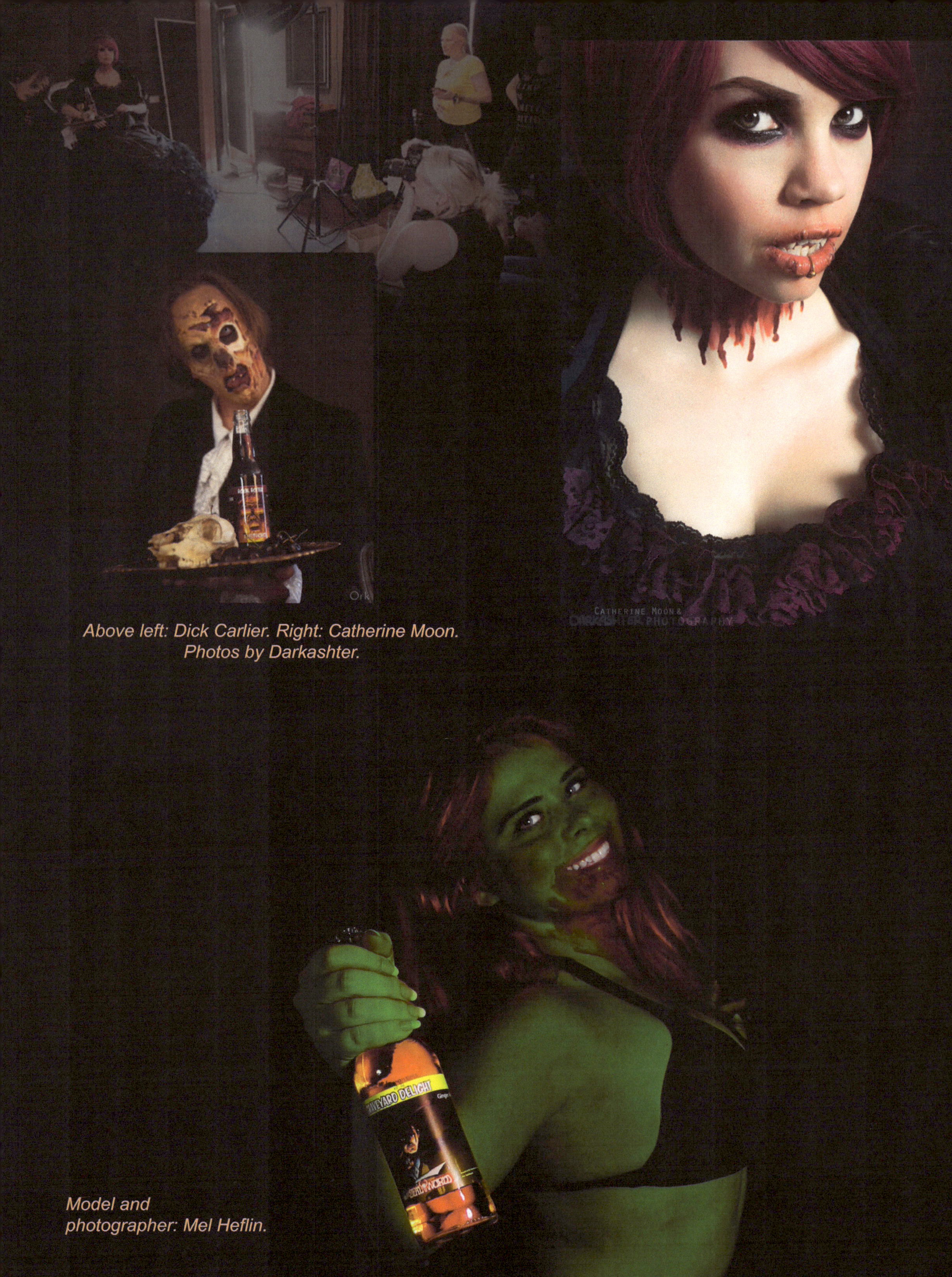

Above left: Dick Carlier. Right: Catherine Moon.
Photos by Darkashter.

Model and
photographer: Mel Heflin.

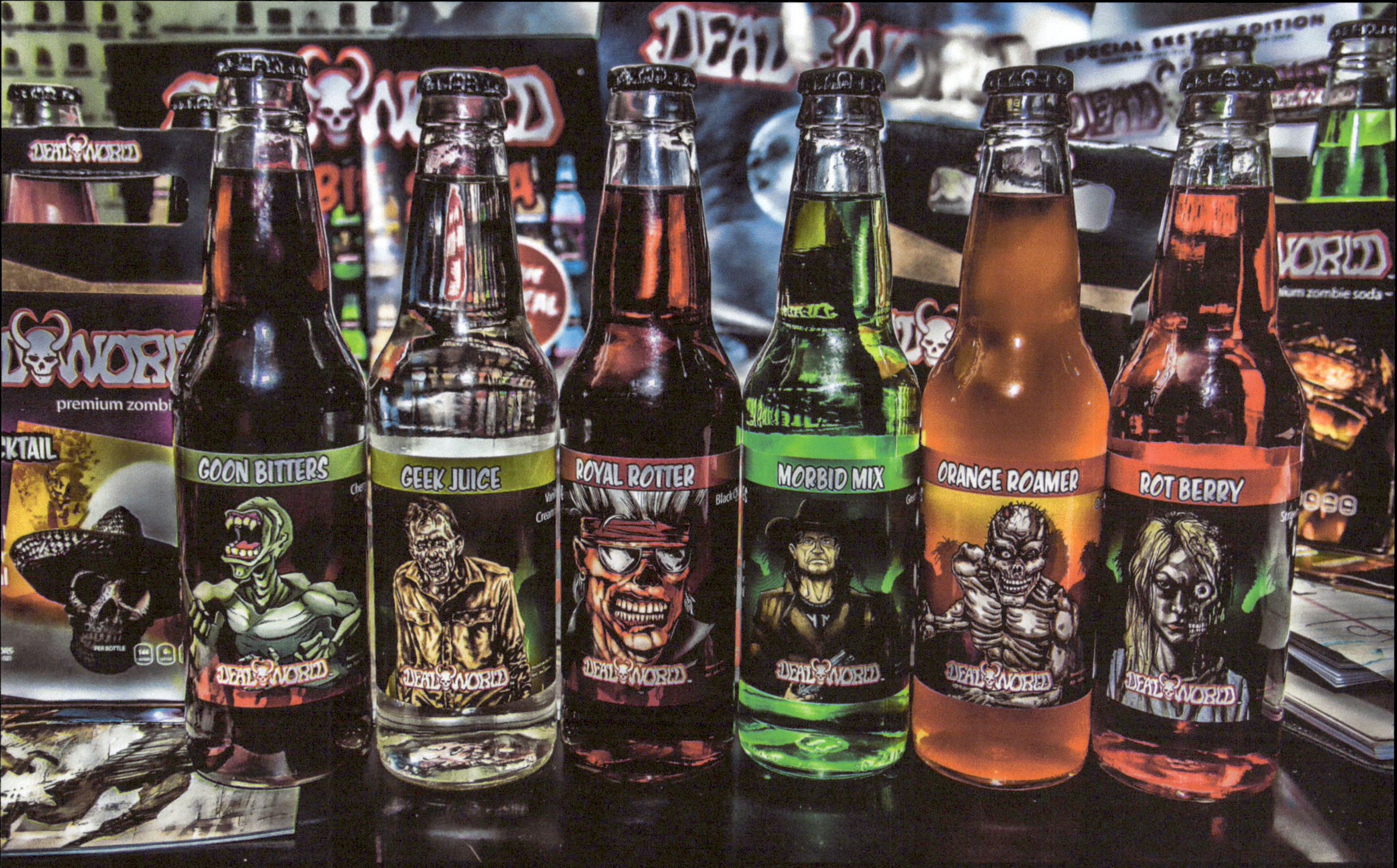

Above: Photo by Robert Richards. Below photos: Jim Bevins and Dalton Brown, photos by Bonnie Brown.

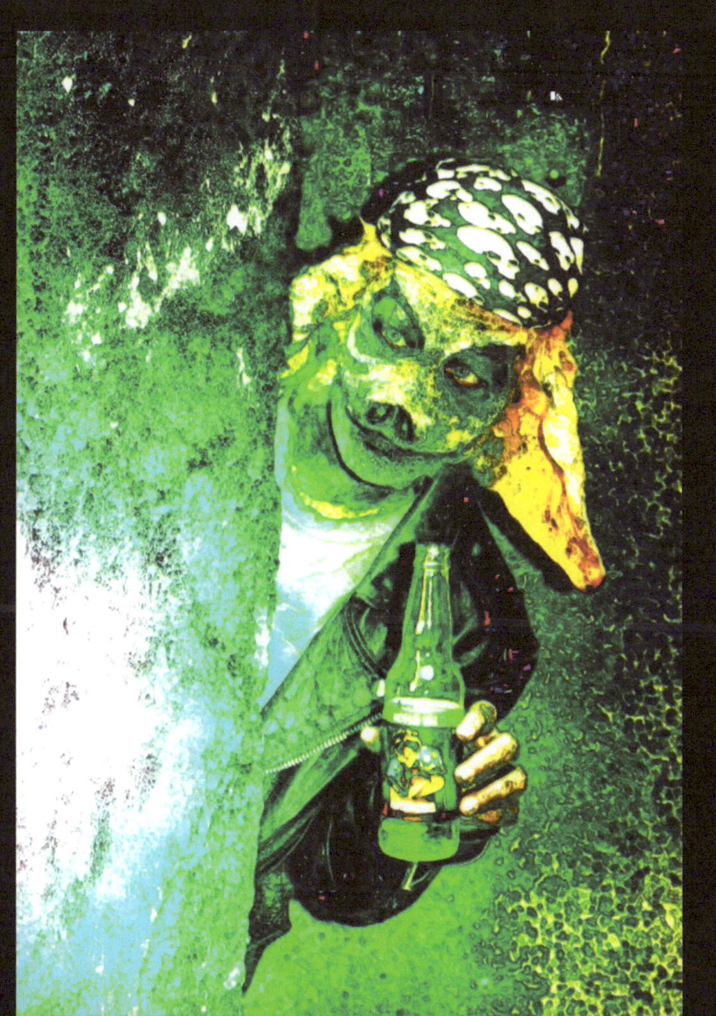

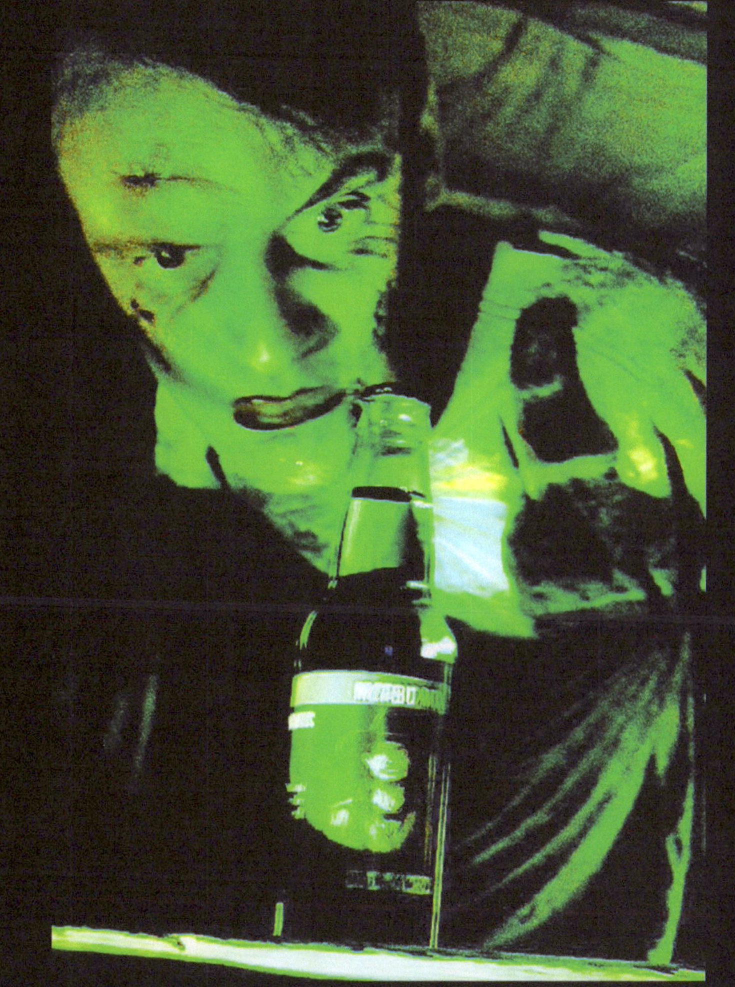

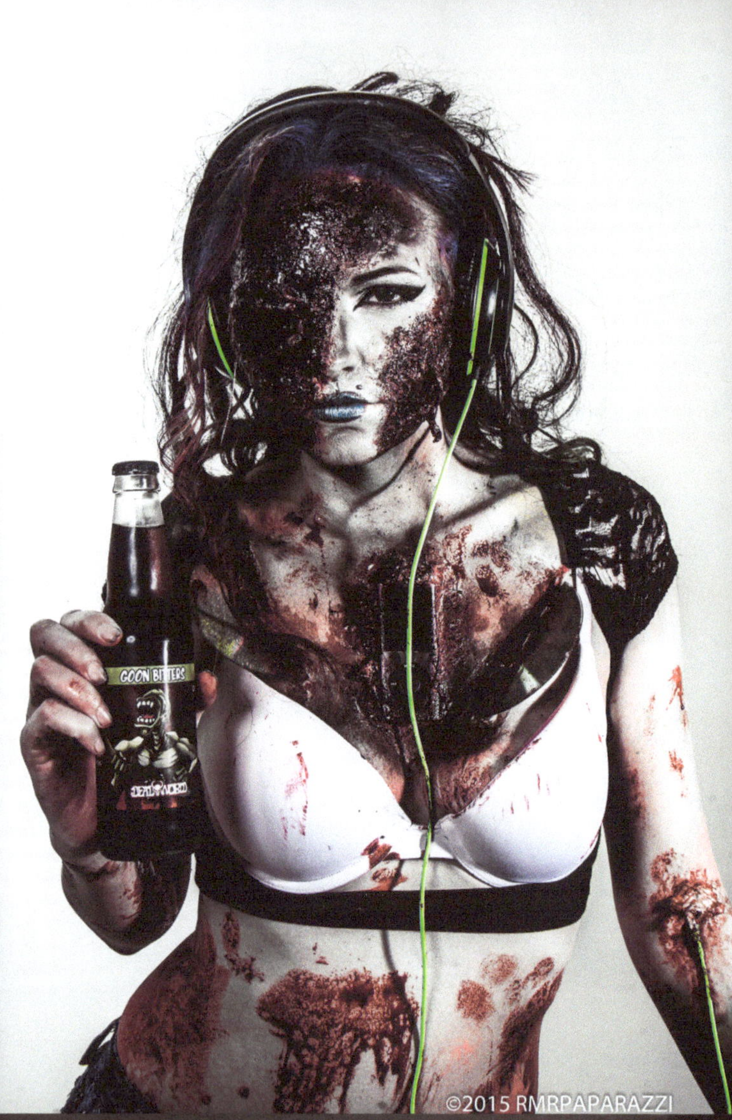

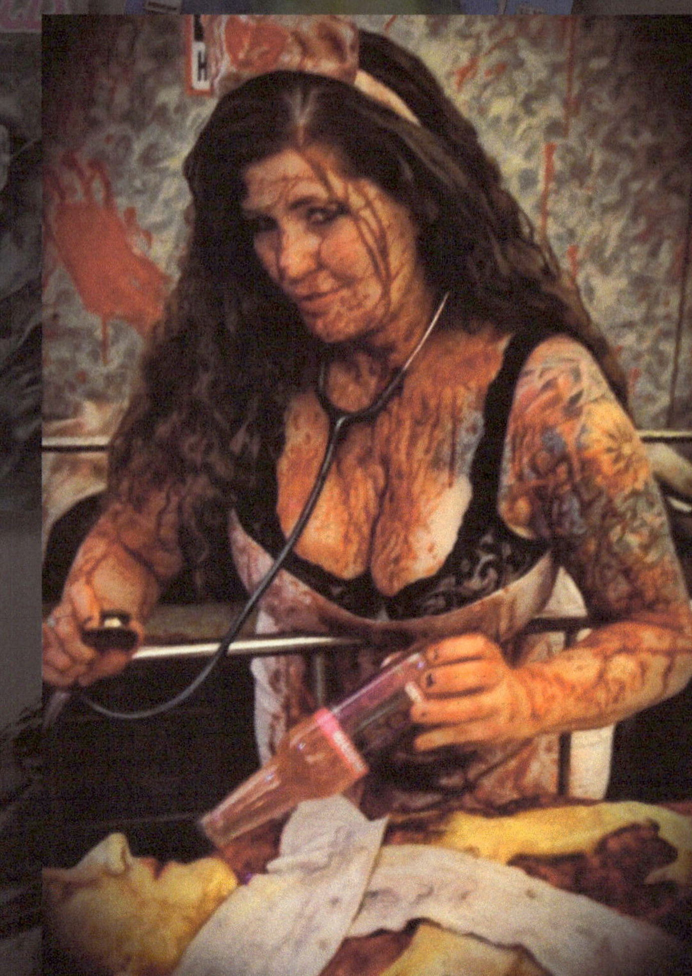

Above: Janet Brickhouse, photo by Bonnie Brown.
Below: Jim Bevins, photo by Dee Miller Owens.

Above and below: Photos by Robert Richards.

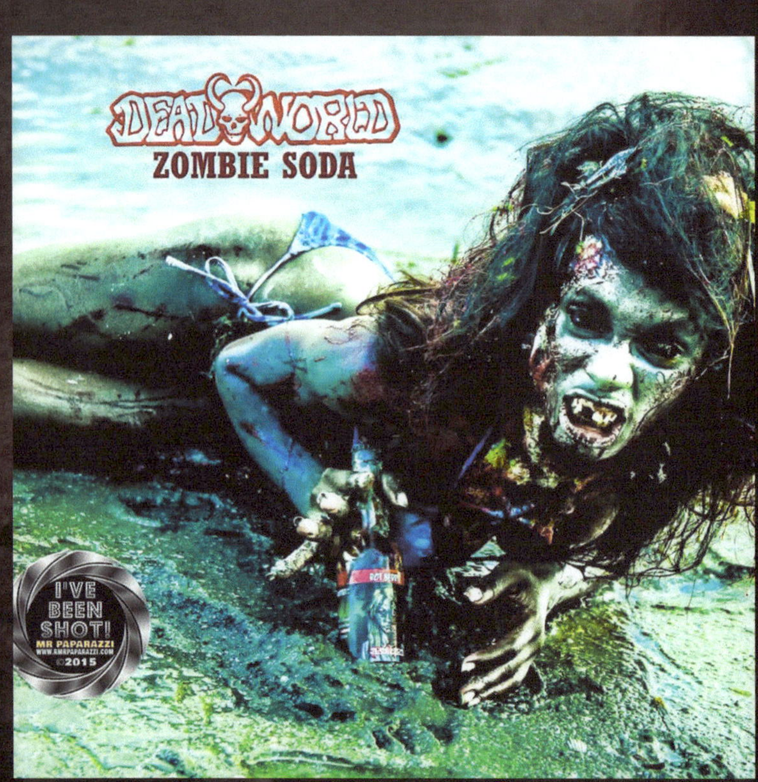

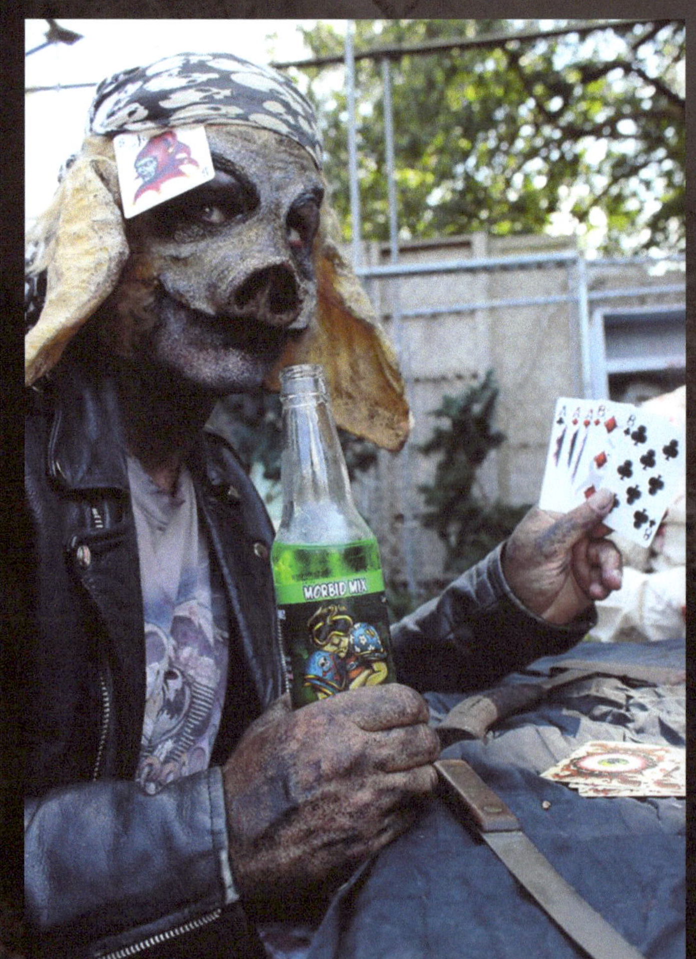

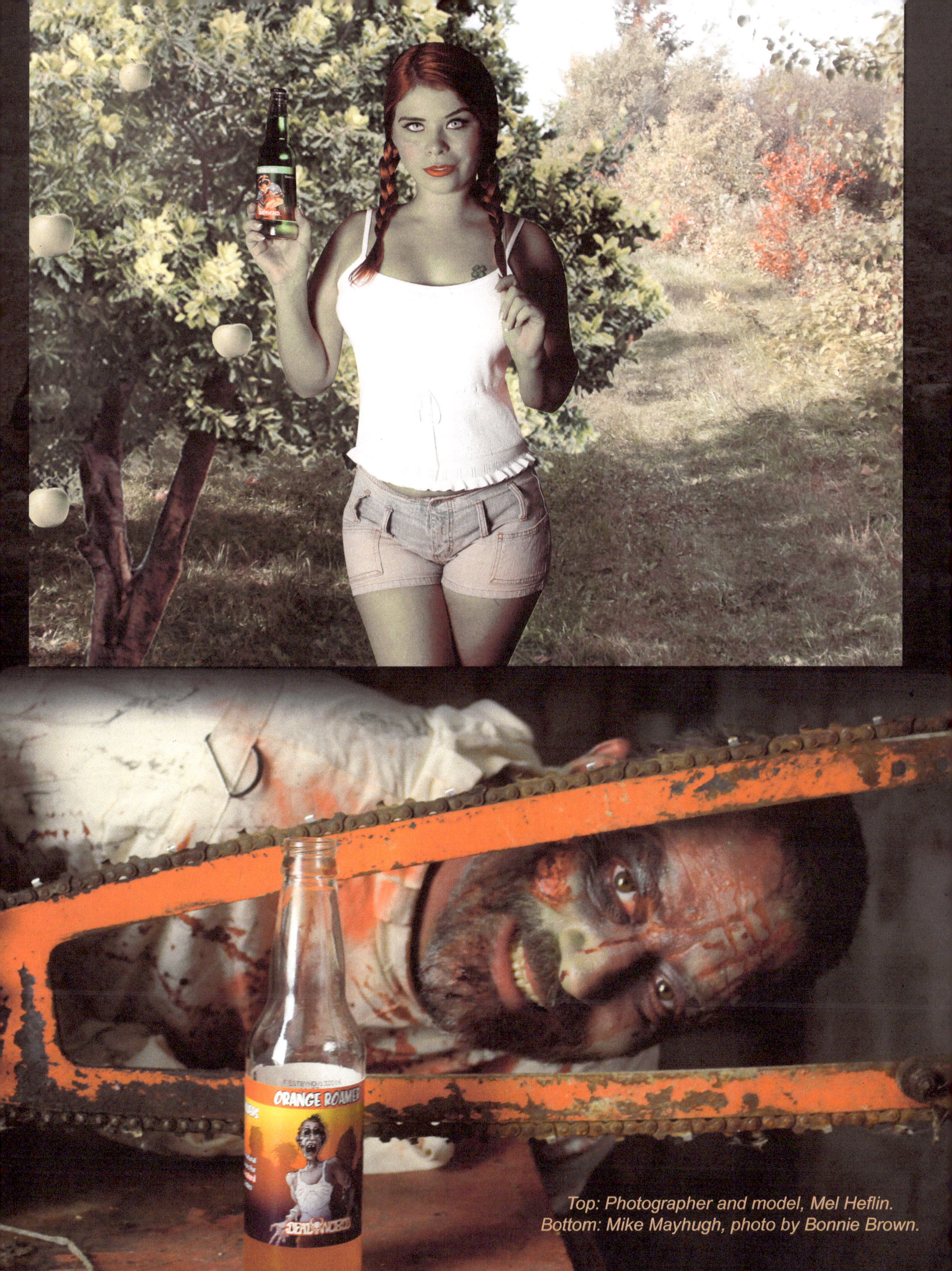

Top: Photographer and model, Mel Heflin.
Bottom: Mike Mayhugh, photo by Bonnie Brown.

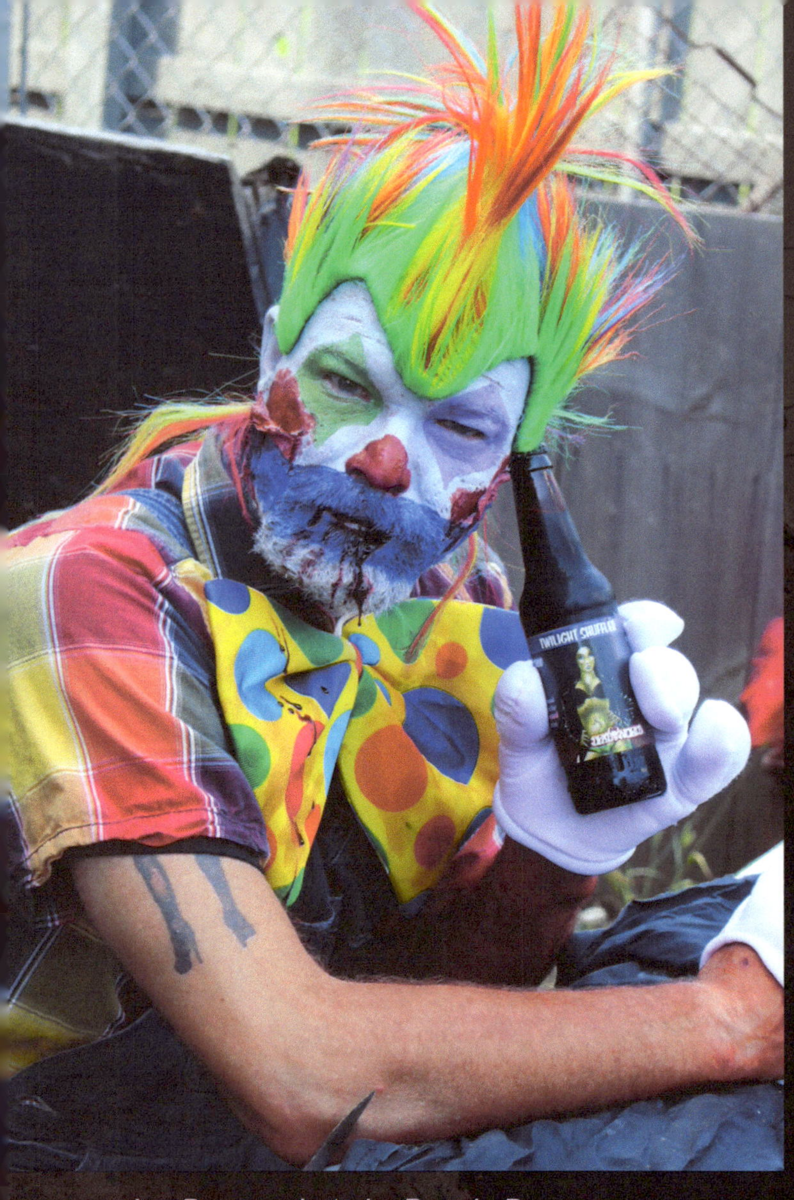

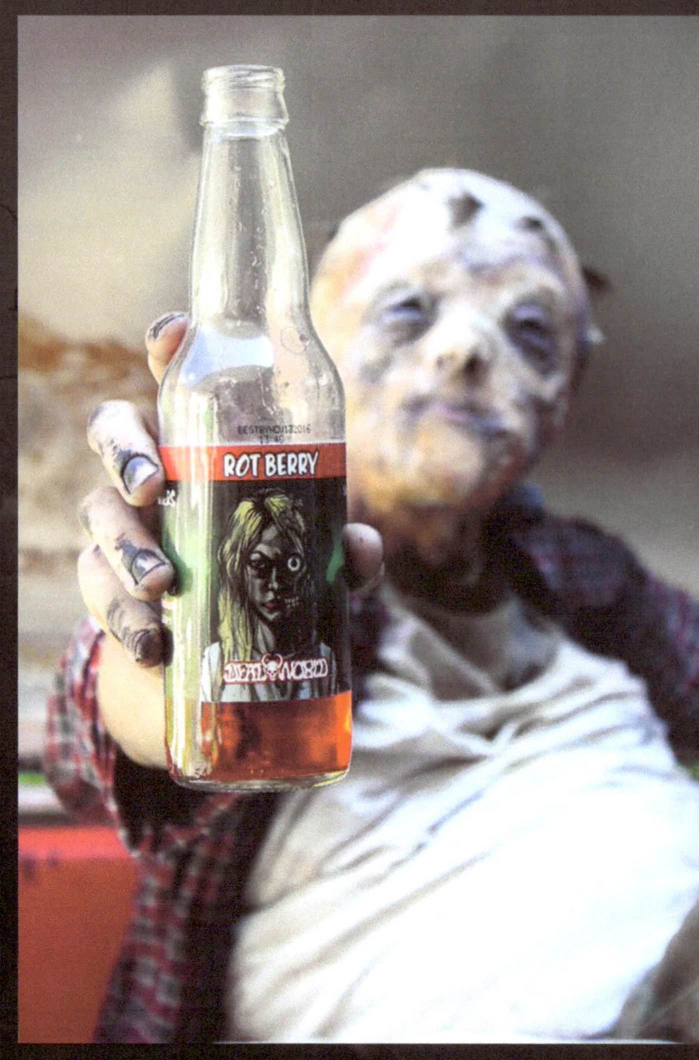

Kyle Dickman, photo by Dee Miller Owens.

Jon Brown, photo by Bonnie Brown.

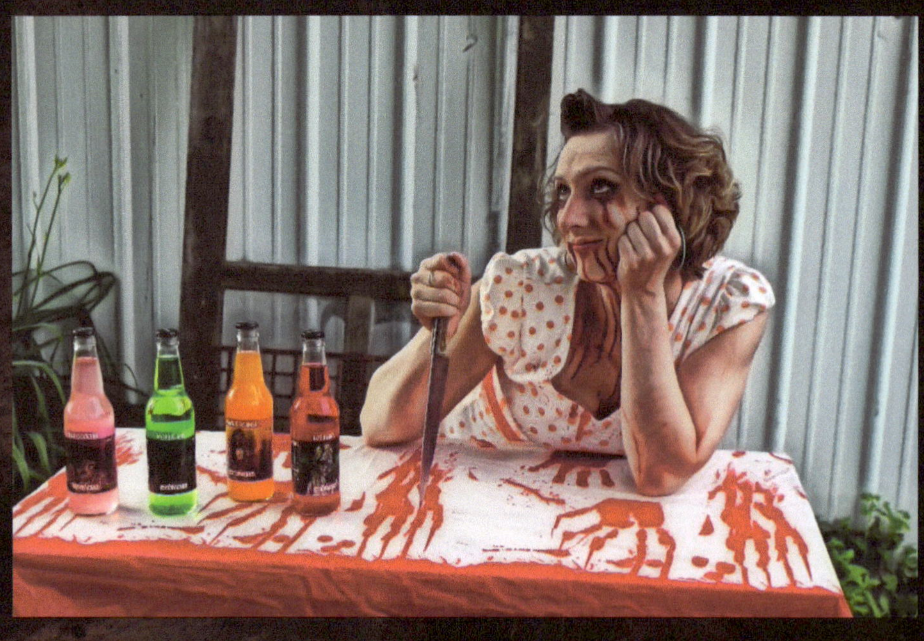

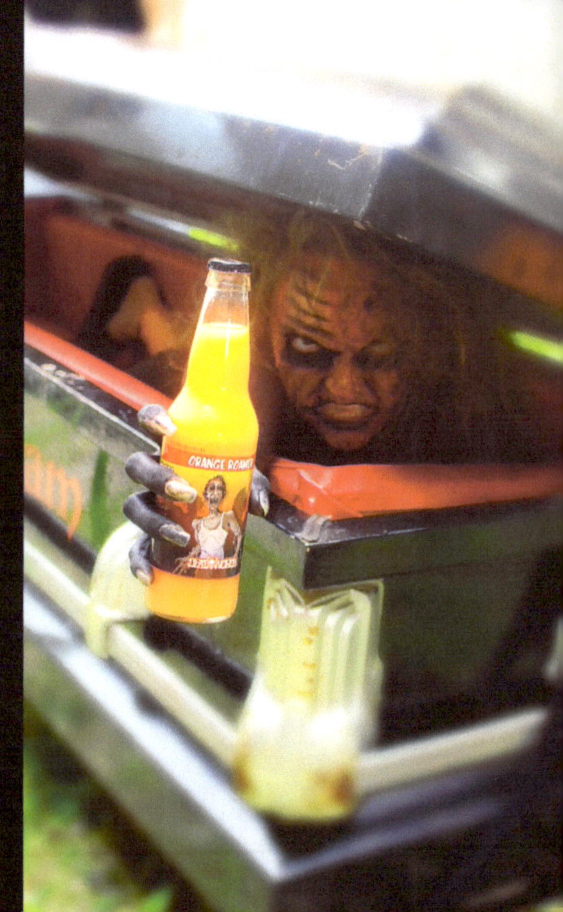

Above: Rose Tennison, photo by Bonnie Brown.
Right: Natasha Smith, photo by Bonnie Brown.

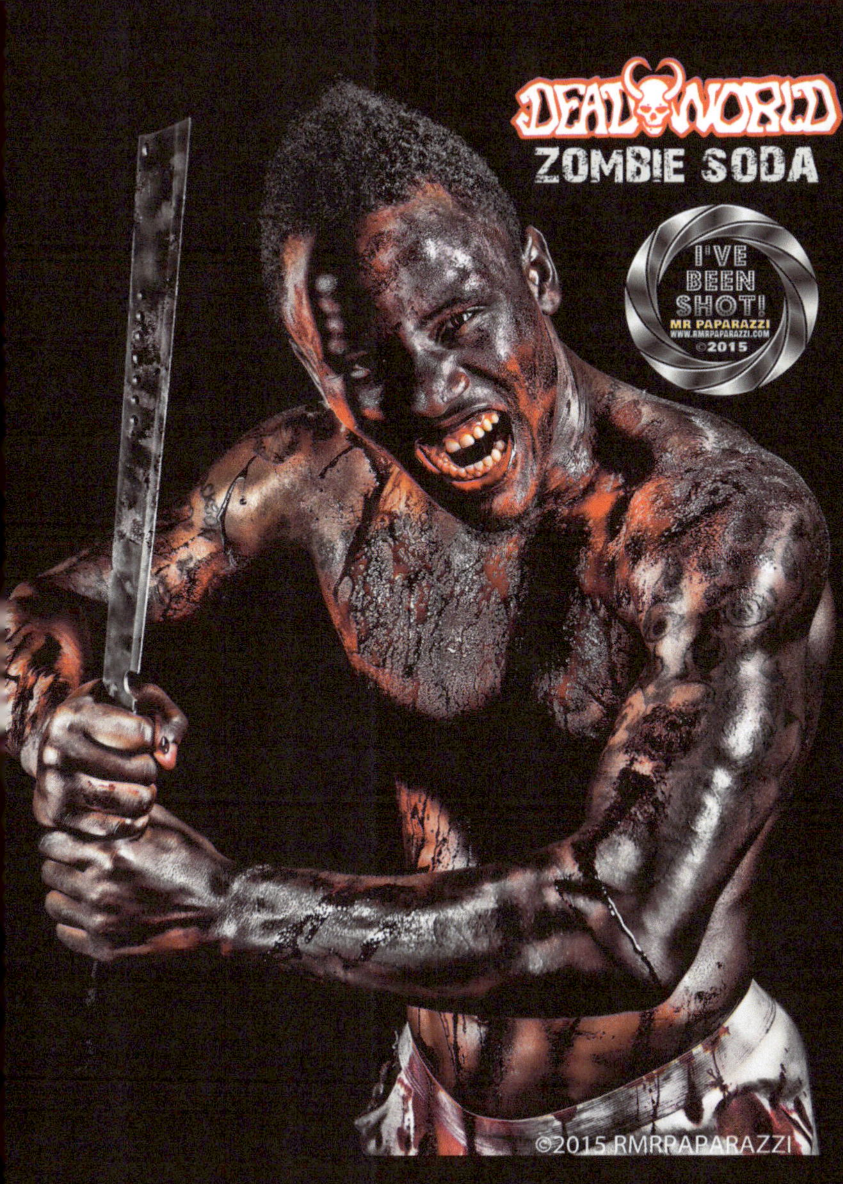

Above and below: Photo by Robert Richards.

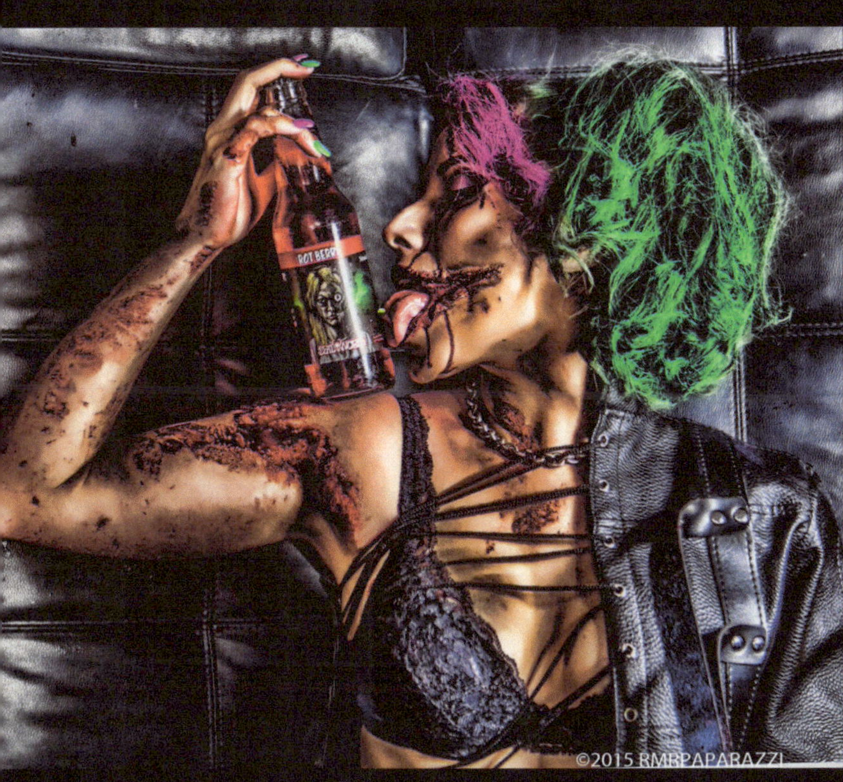

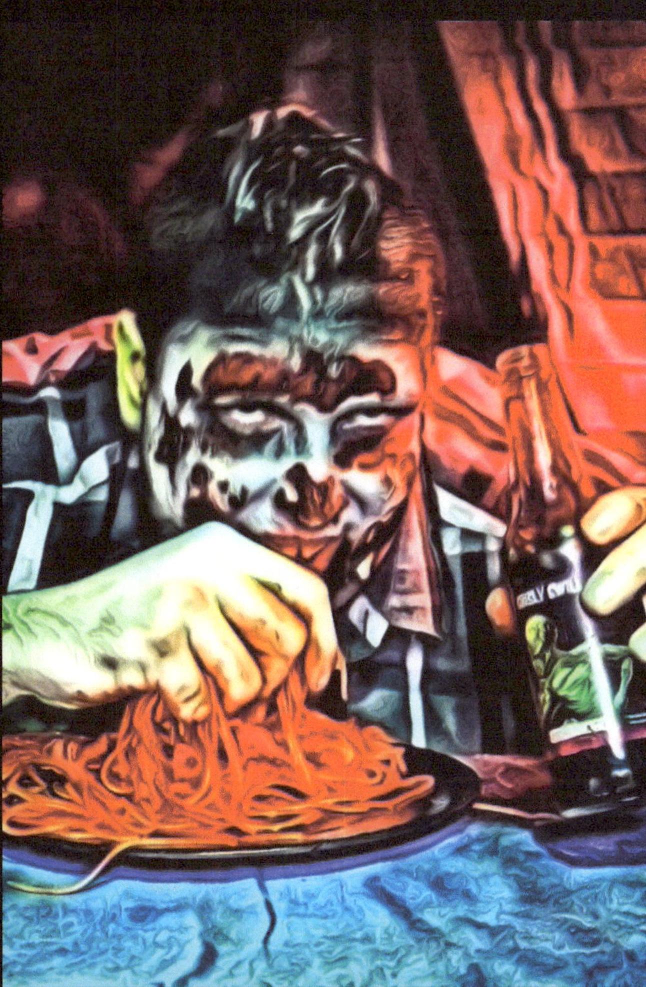

Above: Zach Cousino, photo by Bonnie Brown.
Below: Natasha Smith, with art by Jon Bishop.
Photo by Bonnie Brown.

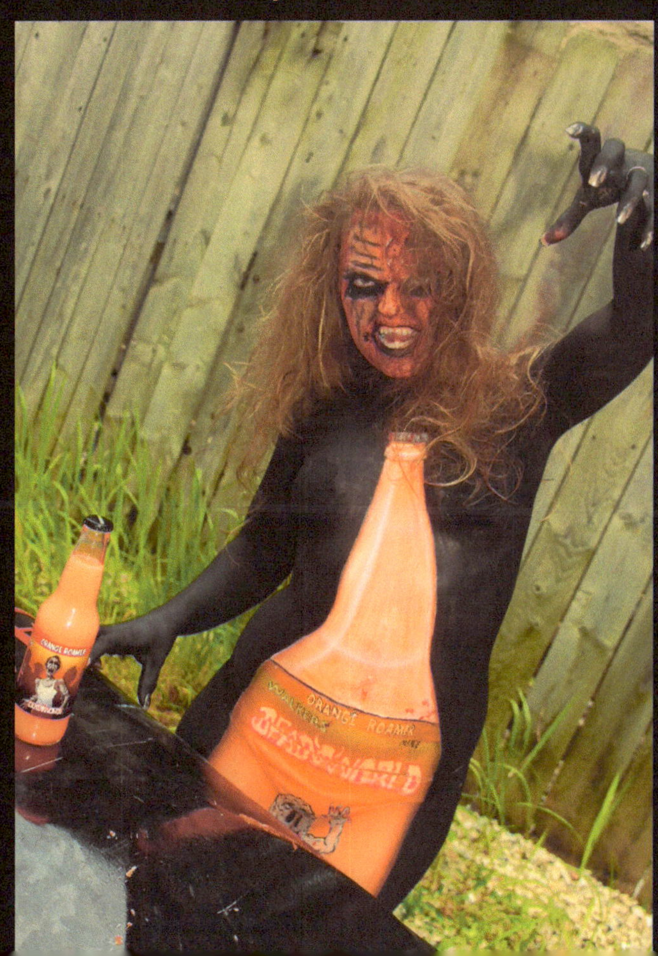

POTATO CHIPS

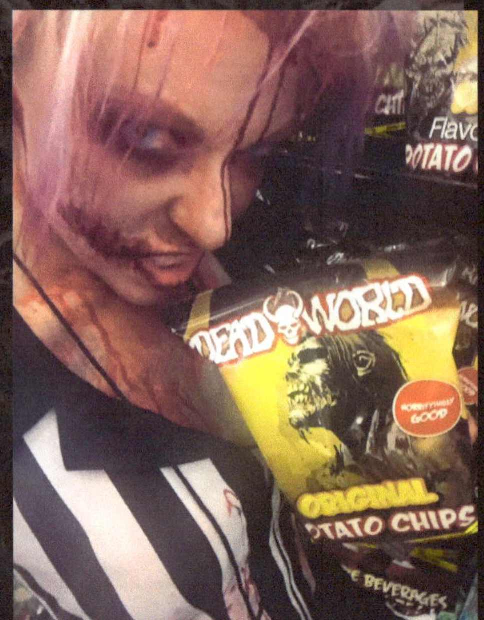

Heather Nance.

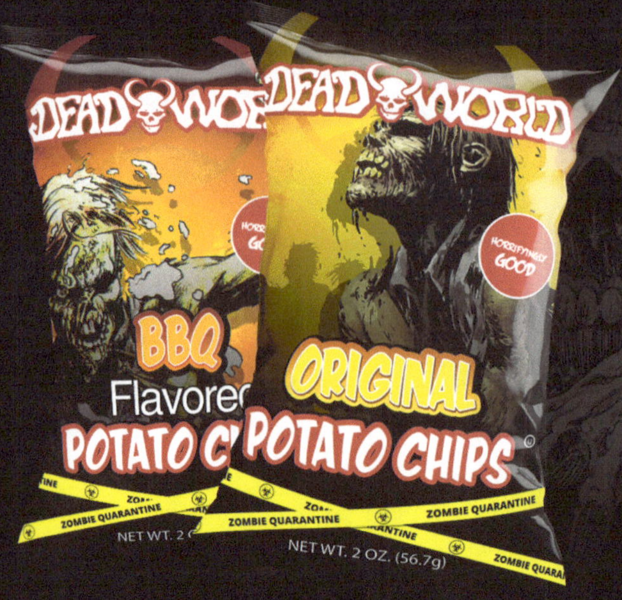

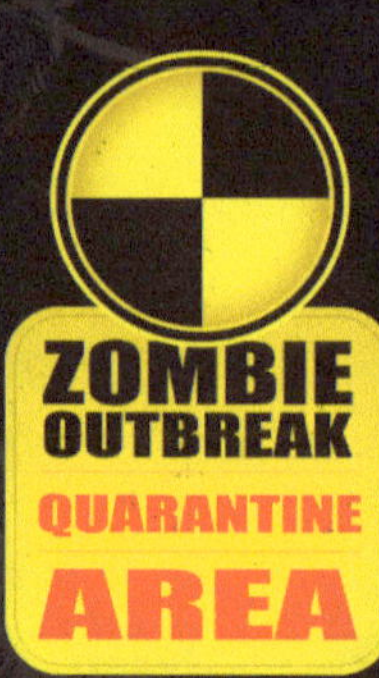

Promo design by Jim Blakeslee.

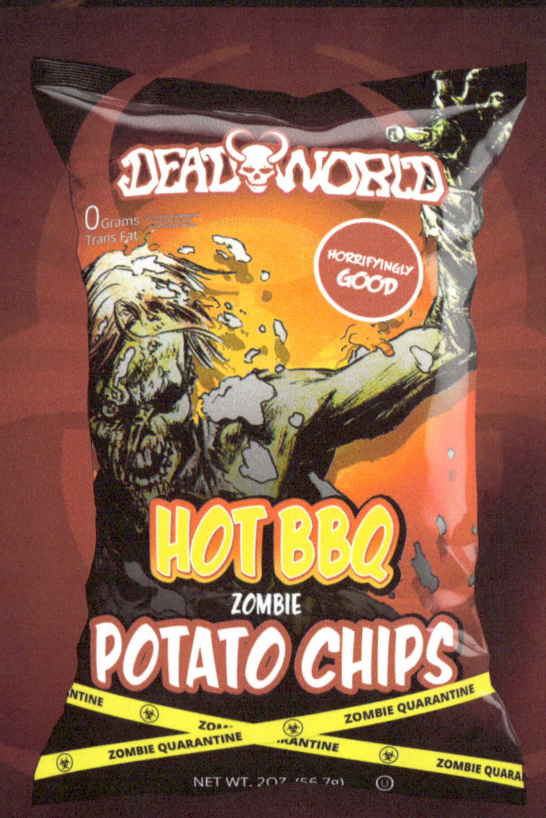

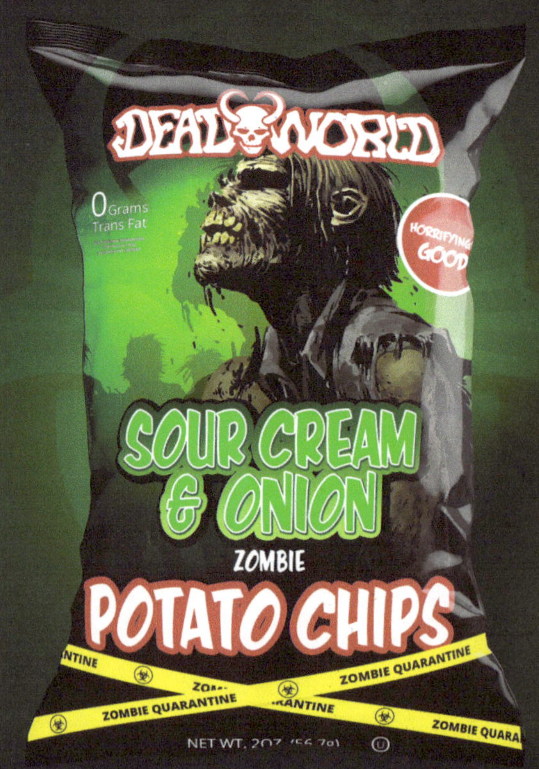

Design by Jim Blakeslee.

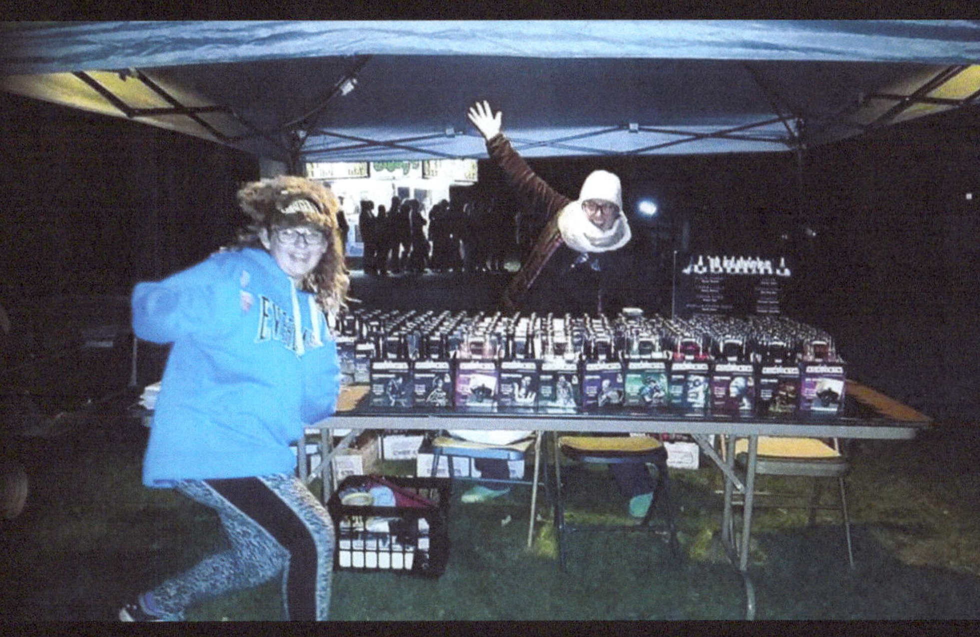

Alaina and Janelle Powers at Screams in the Dark Haunt. Photo by Brittany Nelson.

Freddie Novak.

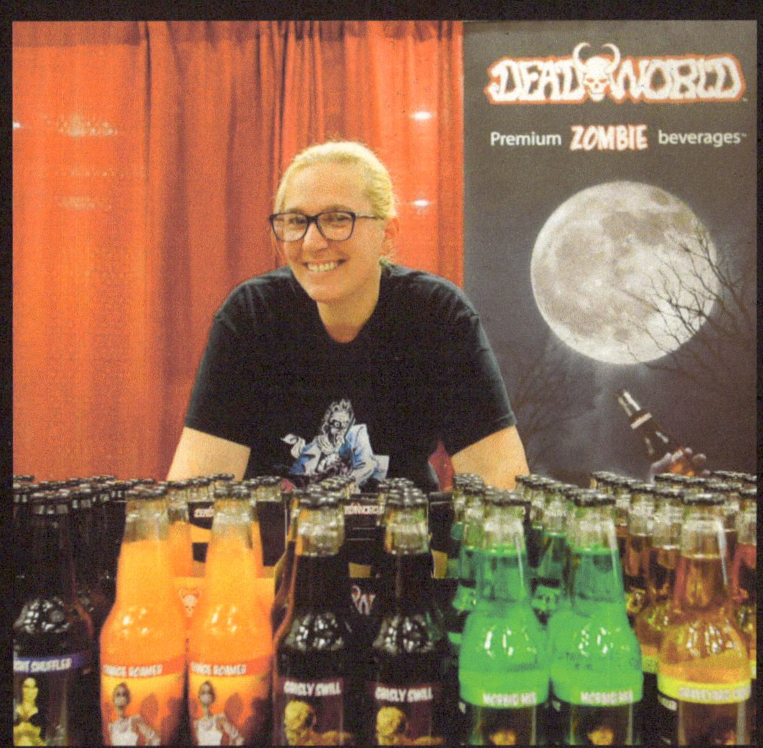

Janelle Powers at Chicago Frights. Photo by Paul Burke.

Freddie Novak and Heather Nance at NACS Show.

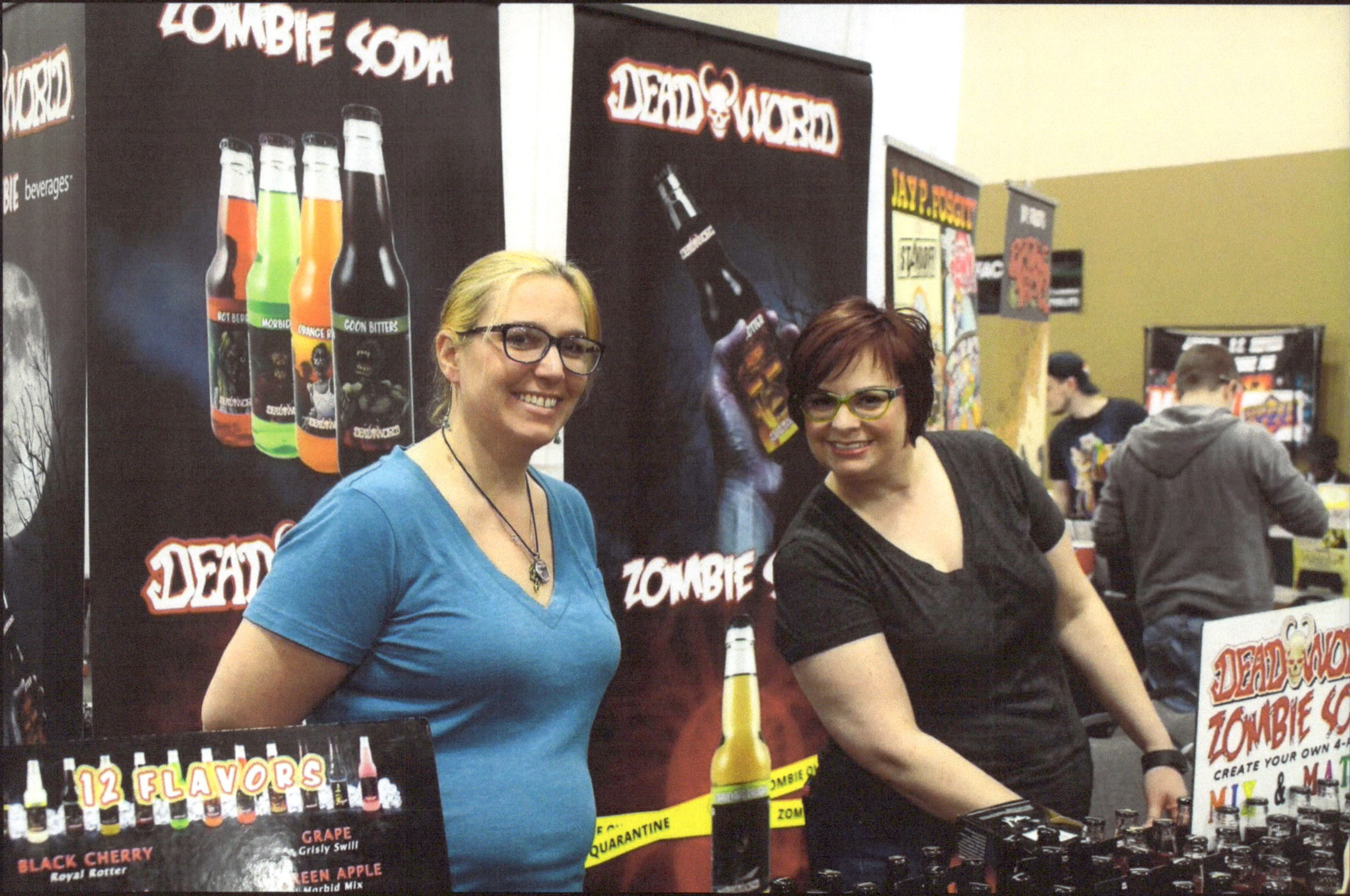

Janelle Powers and Janelle Box in Toledo. Photo by Bonnie Brown.

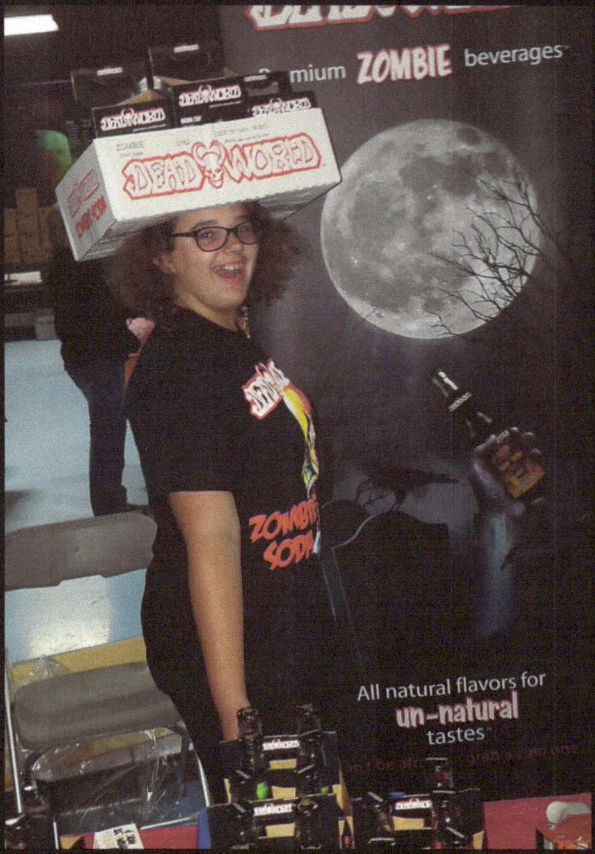

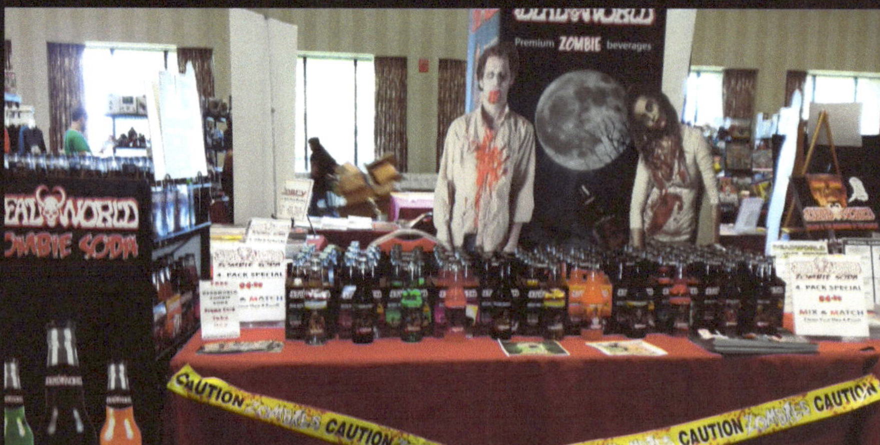

Above: Northville Nightmares Convention. Below: Wayne Car Show.

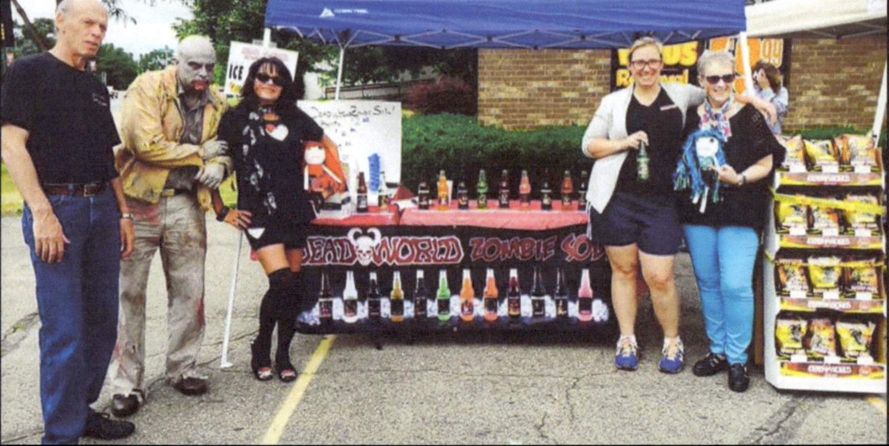

Alaina wearing the new DW Box Hat at the Haunted Garage Sale.

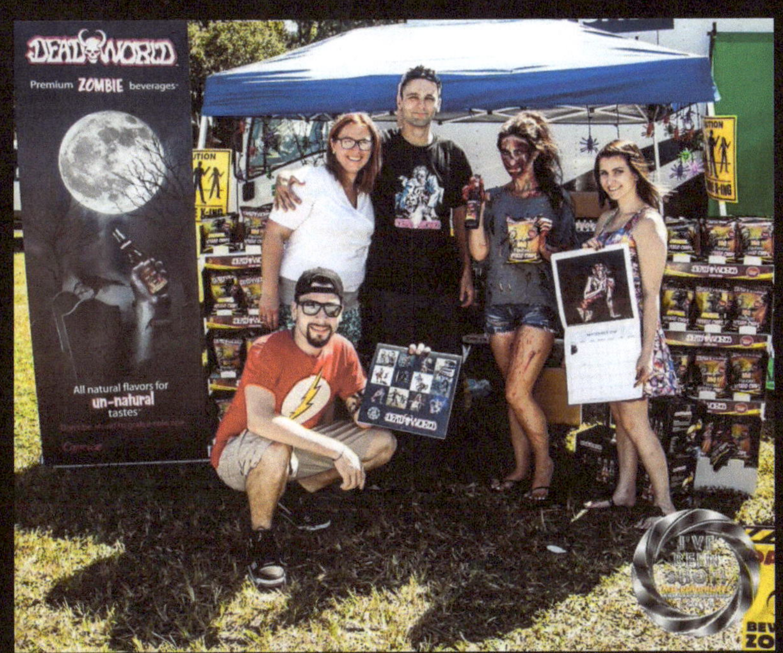

Janelle, Joe Davis, Ace Yvonne, Kylie and Shannon at Lakeland Zombiefest.

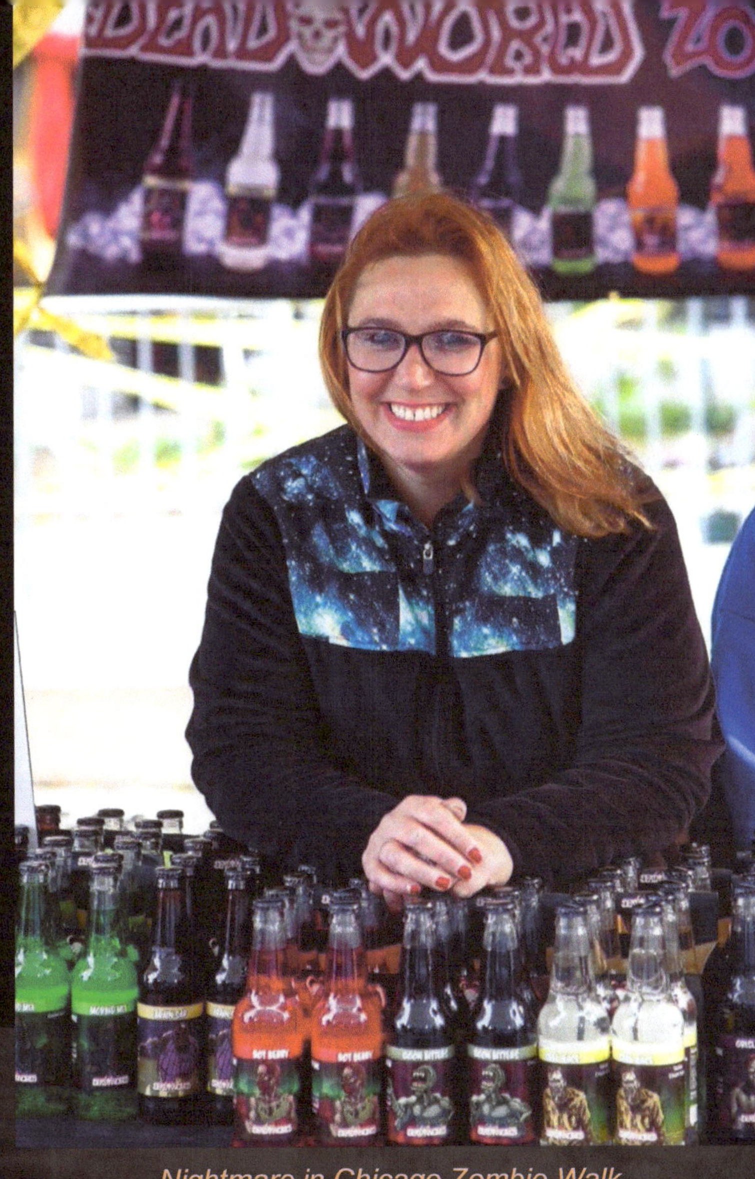

Nightmare in Chicago Zombie Walk. Photo by Bonnie Biksacky.

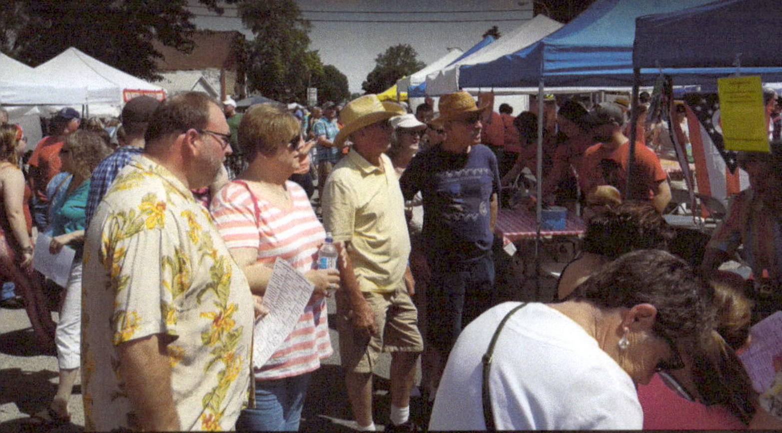

Above: Homer Soda Festival.
Below: Zombie Bride at Chicago Frights. Photo by Janelle Powers.

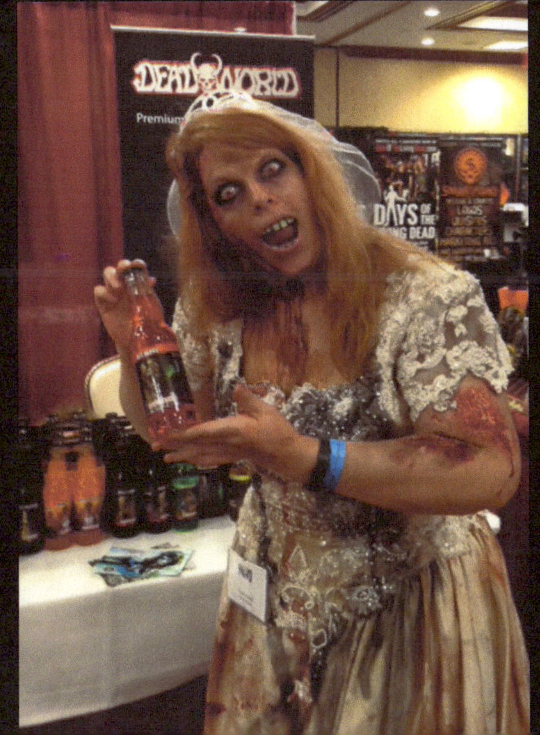

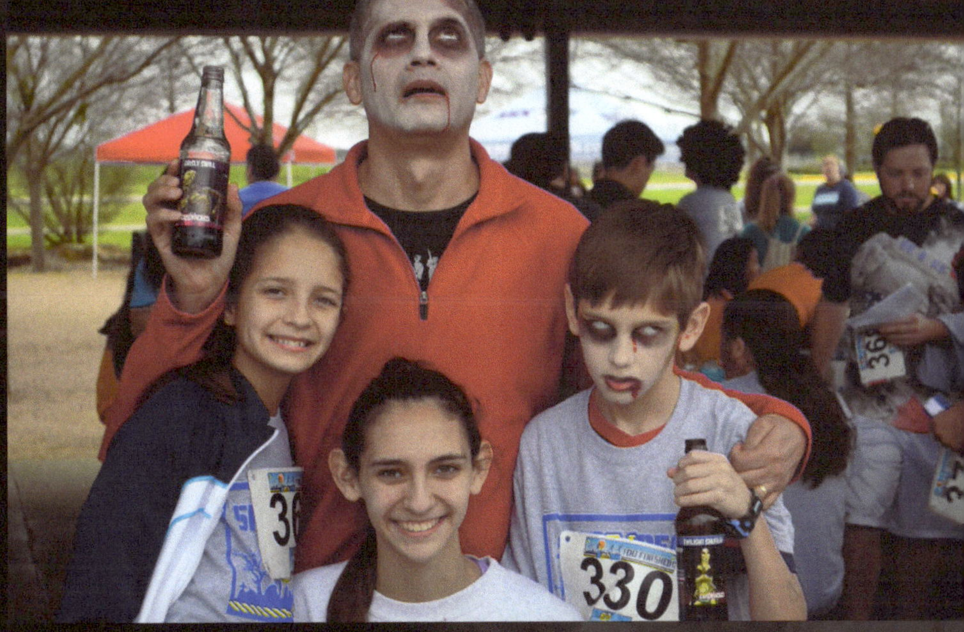

Zombie Family in Houston. Photo by Jim Blakeslee.

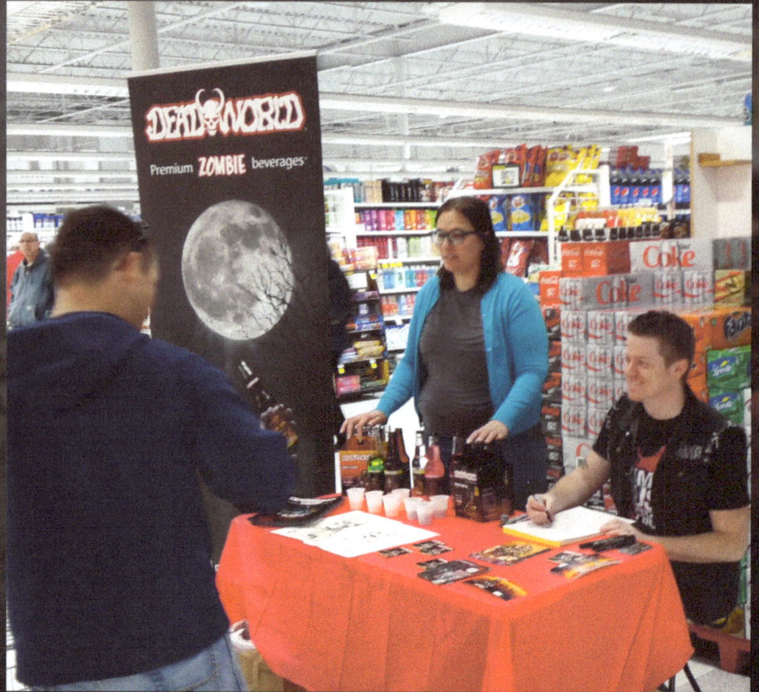

The 1st sampling at Hollywood Market with Joshua Werner.

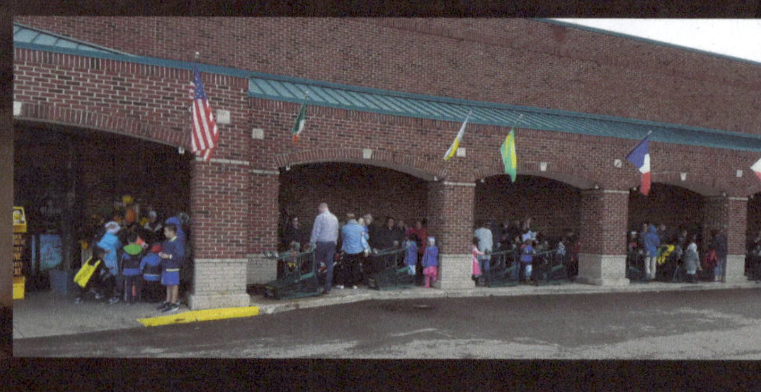

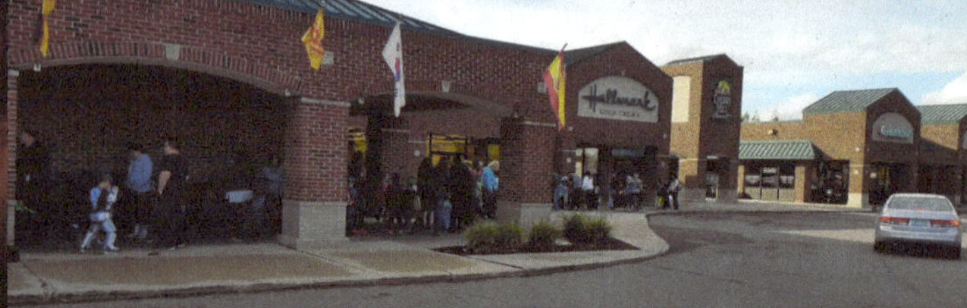

The crowd in line to get inside Hollywood Market.

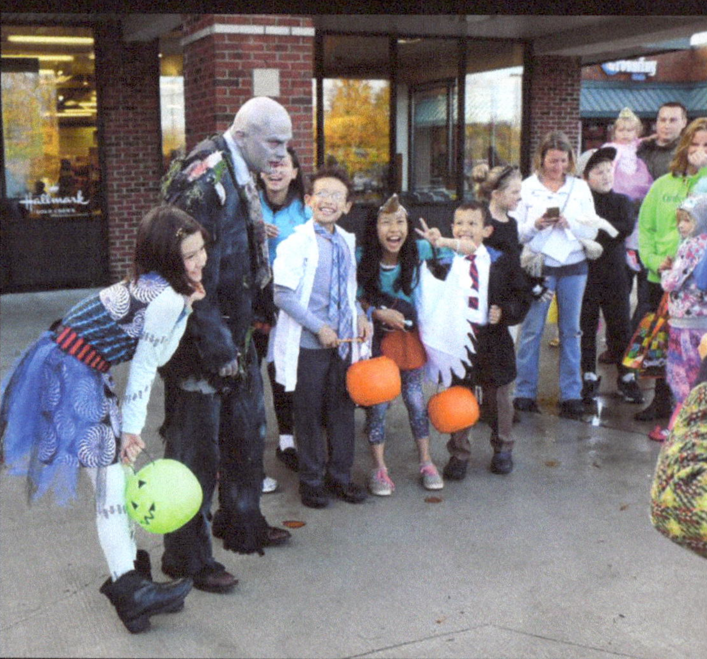

Dedd Fredd with fans. Photo by Paul Burke.

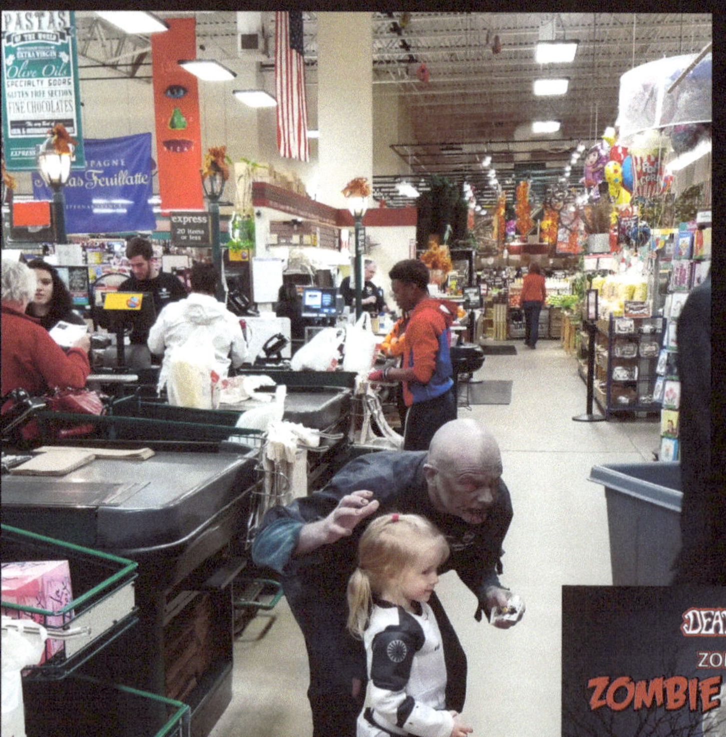

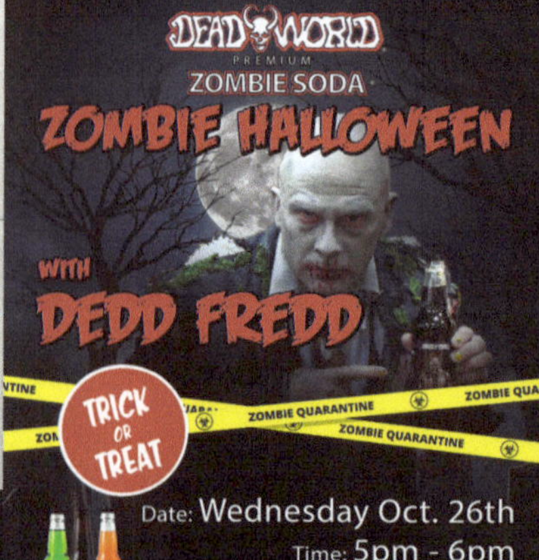

Above: Dedd Fredd poses with a little girl.
Right: Dedd Fredd bags groceries.
Photos by Chelsea Kennedy.

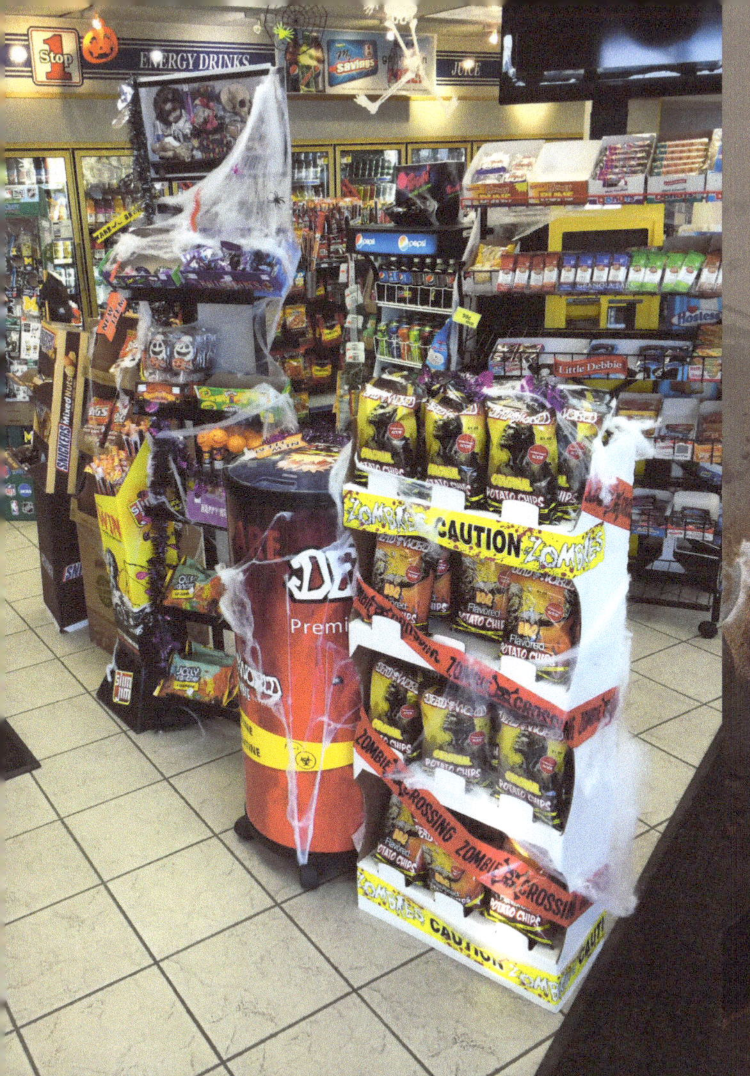

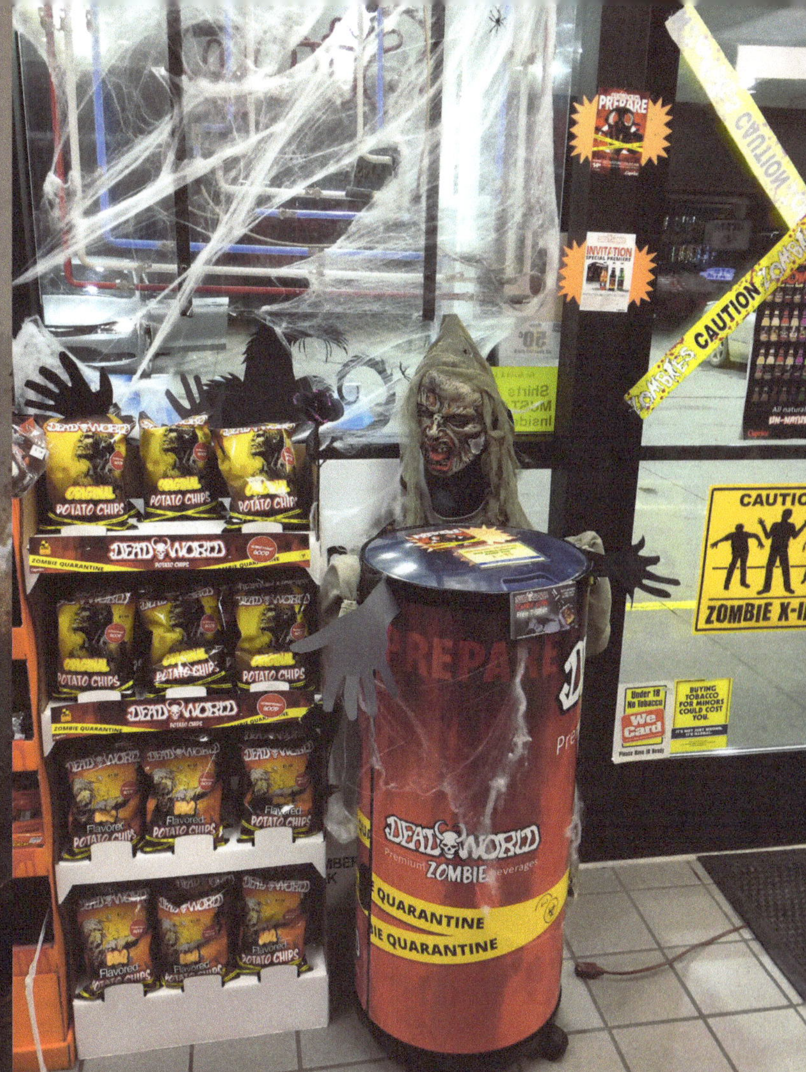

C-Store displays.

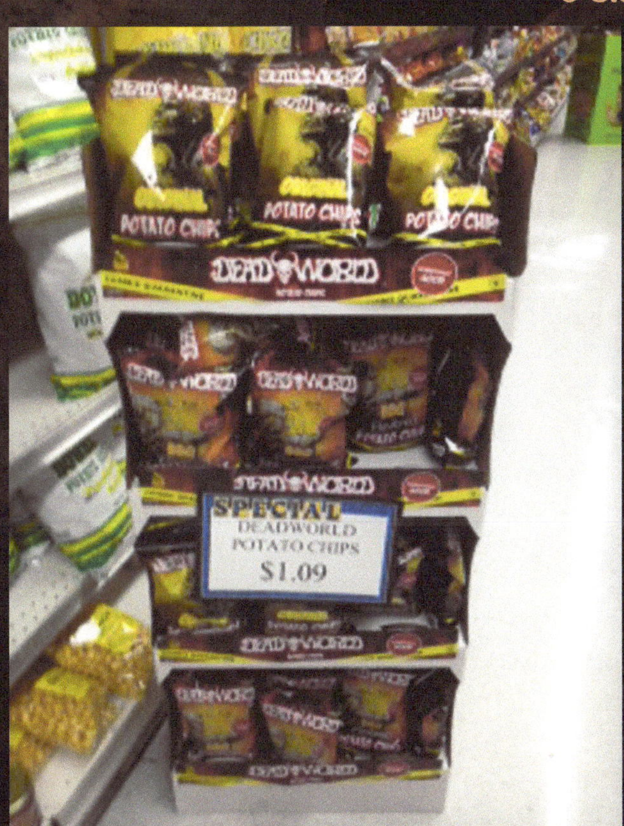

Chips display at Hollywood Market.

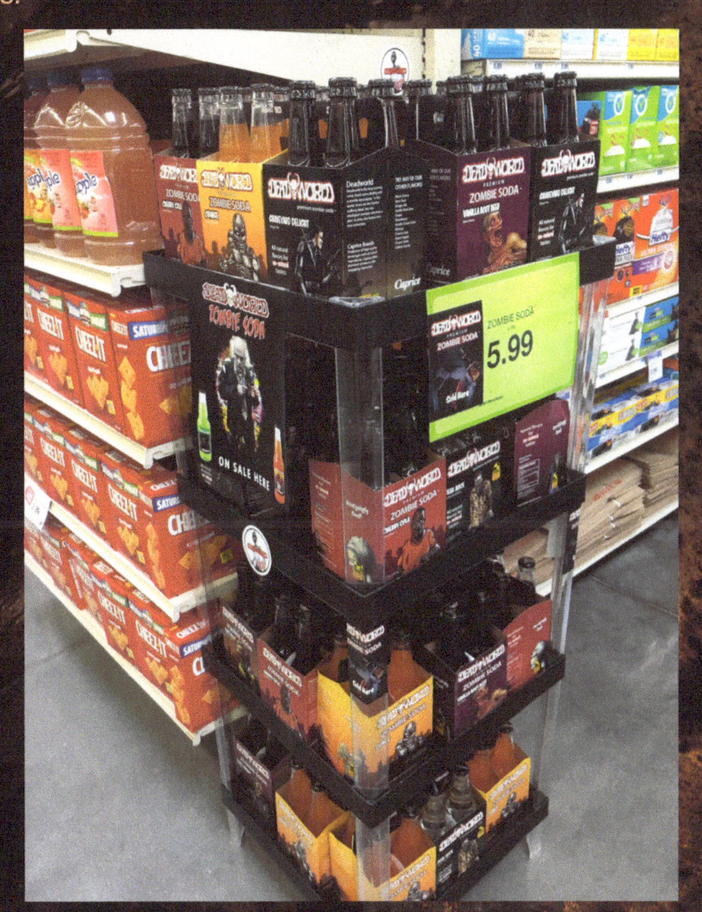

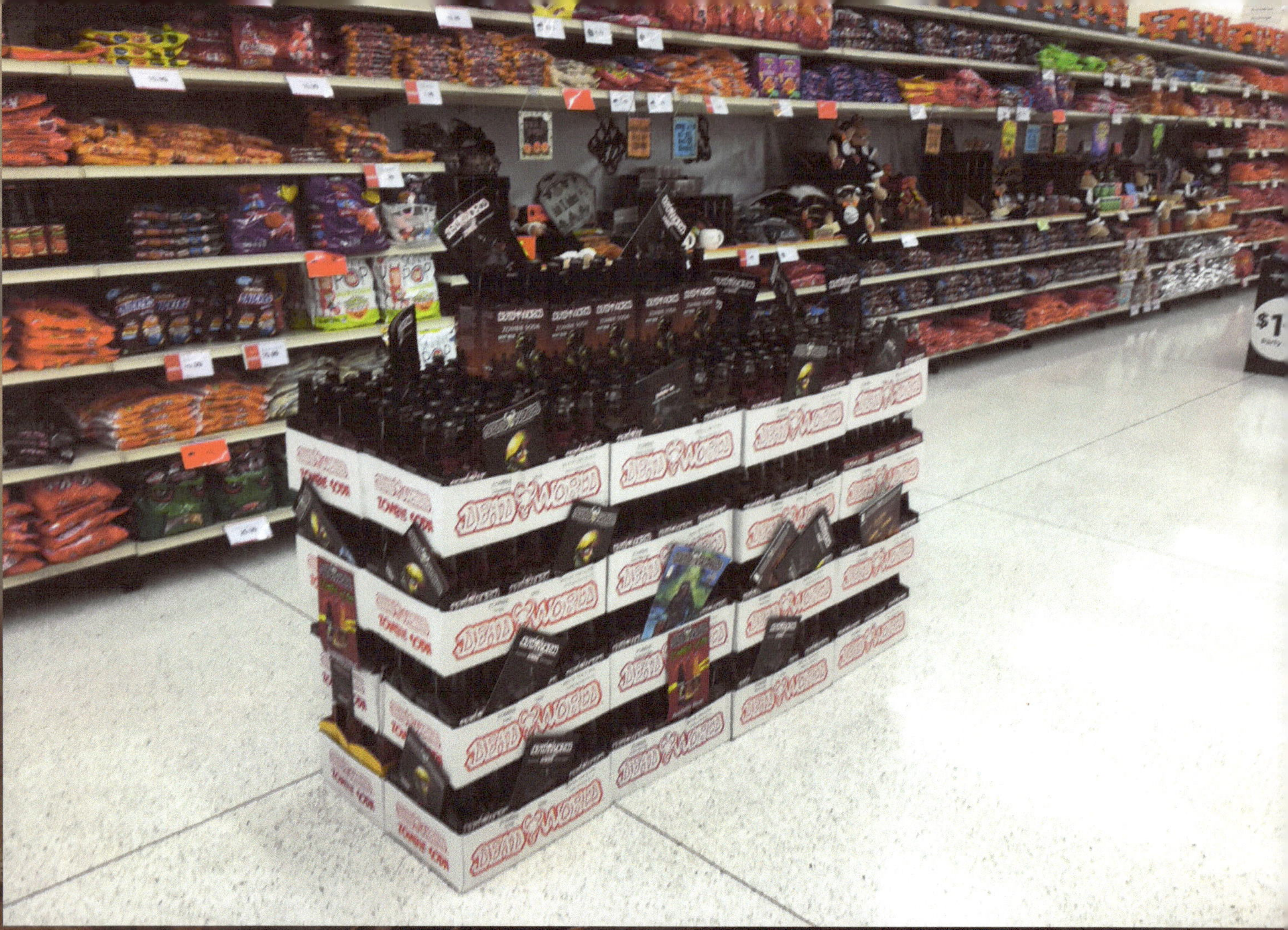

HyVee store displays.

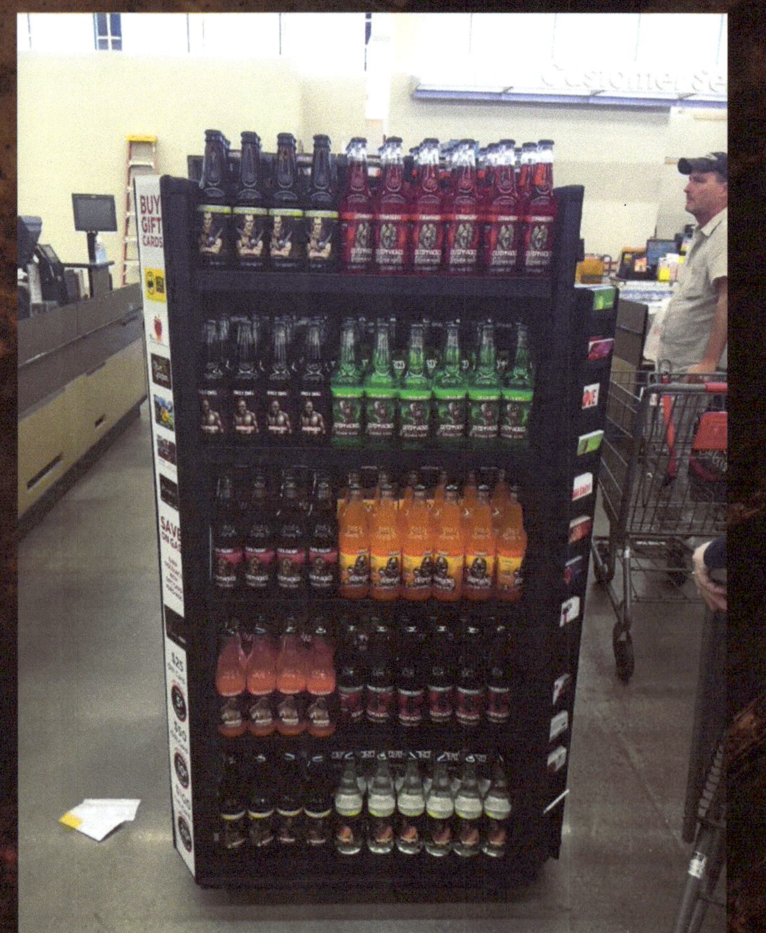

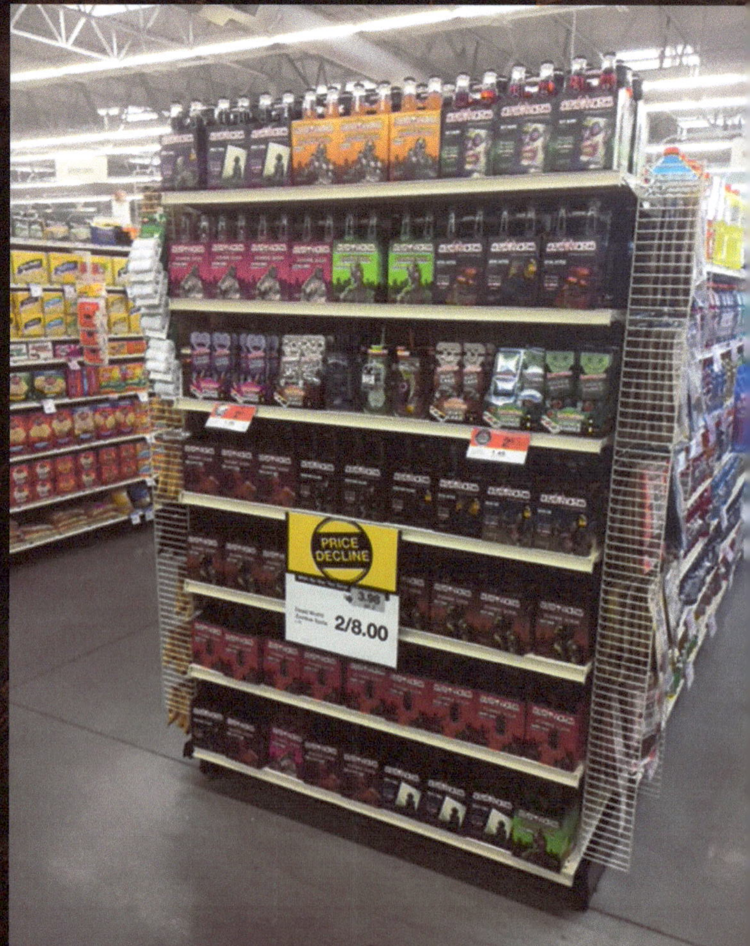

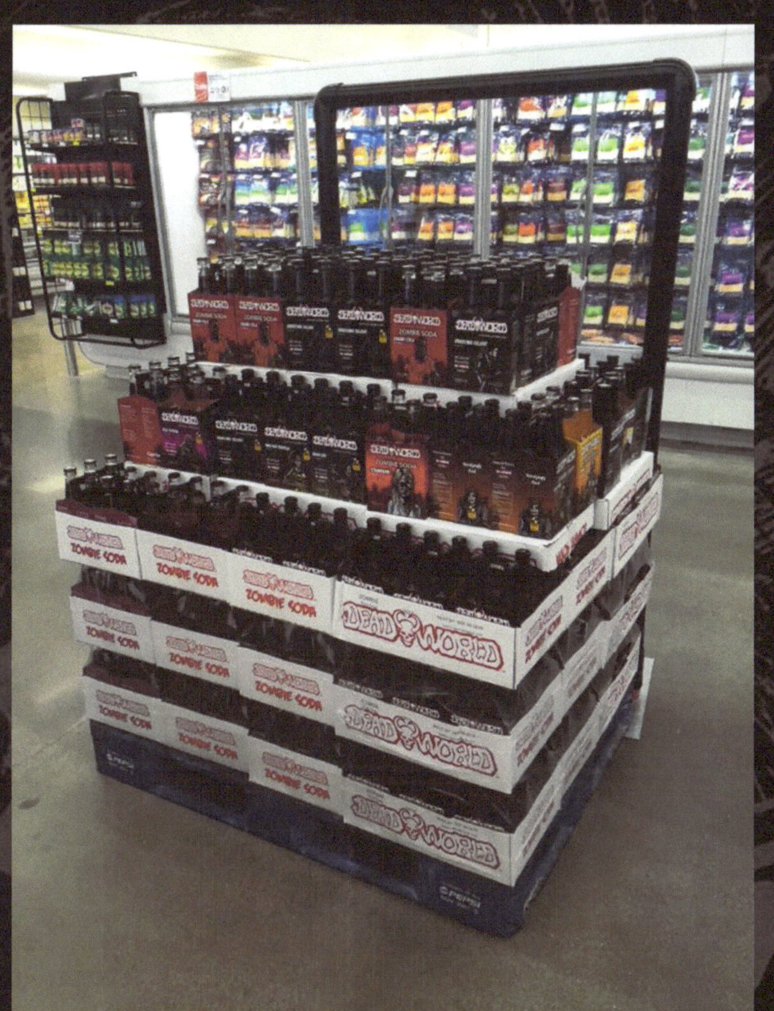

HyVee display.

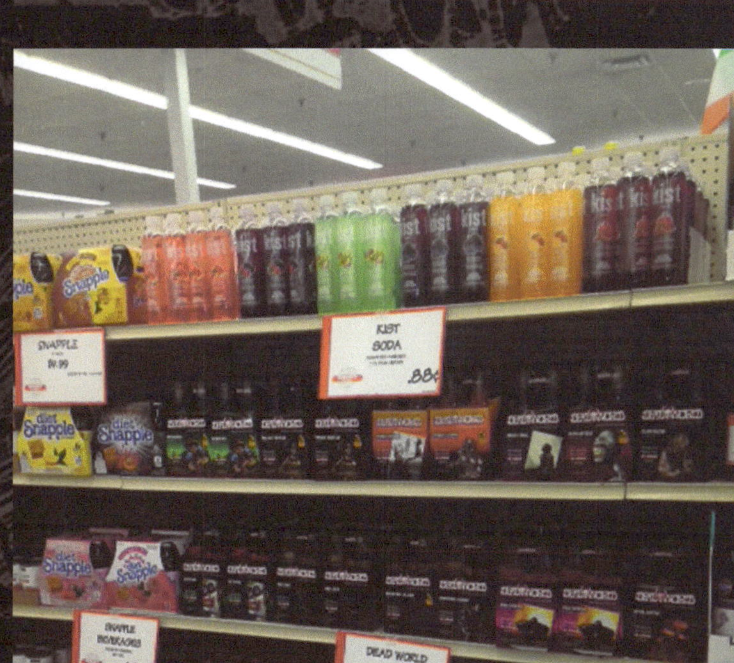

Bueches display.

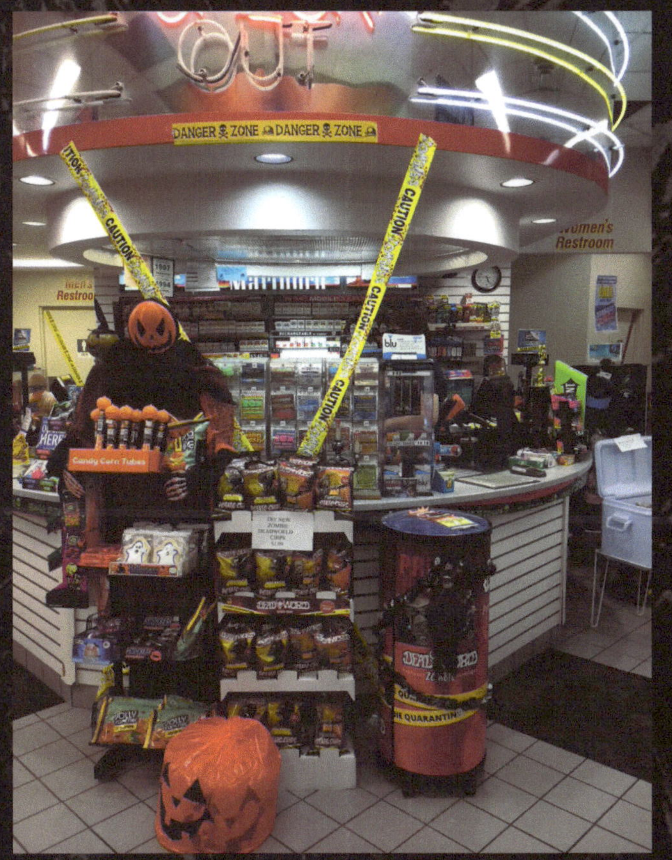

One Stop display.

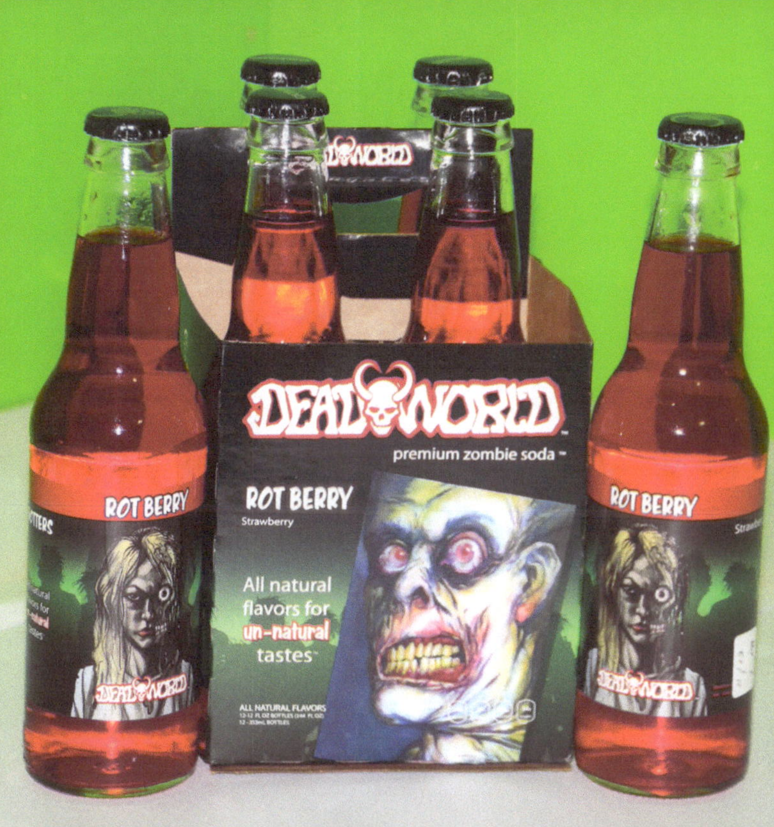

Photo by Jim Blakeslee.

THANK YOU TO EVERYONE WHO HELPED PUT TOGETHER THIS BOOK!
AND TO THE PHOTOGRAPHERS WHO TOOK ALL THESE AMAZING SHOTS!

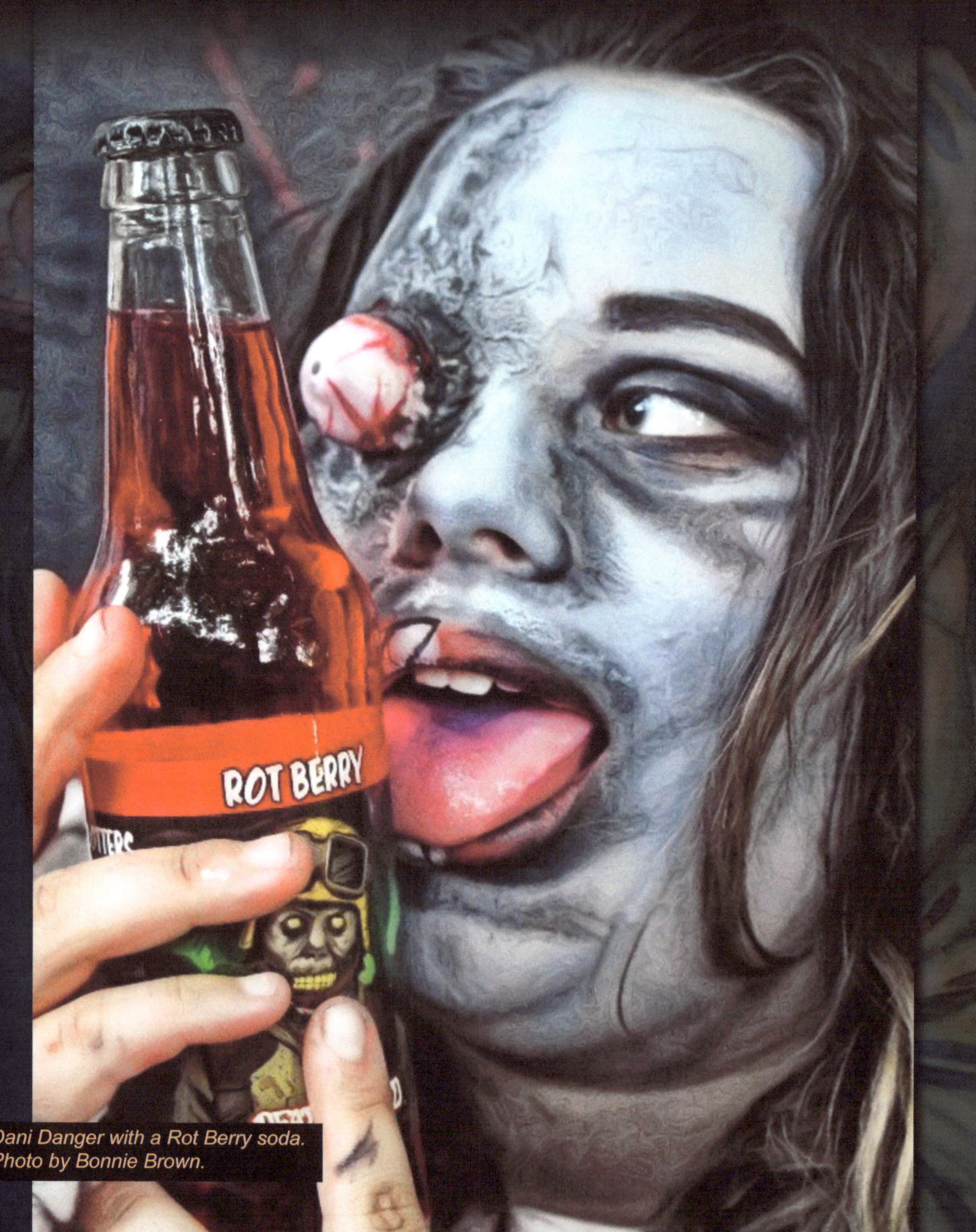

Dani Danger with a Rot Berry soda.
Photo by Bonnie Brown.

CREDITS

Front cover photo by Robert Richards. Back cover photo by Steve Savage Smith.
Page 1 artwork by Joshua Werner, photo by Robert Richards.
Page 2 photo by Dee Miller Owens.
Page 4 artwork by Joshua Werner.
This book contained designs by Jim Blakeslee and photographs by Bonnie Brown, Robert Richards, Steve Savage Smith, Steve Moraca, Mel Heflin, Chelsea Kennedy, Jeff Beach, Janelle Powers, Eric Littlefield, Darkashter, Dee Miller Owens, Paul Burke, Brittany Nelson, Bonnie Biksacky, Jim Blakeslee, and if we missed anyone... We're sorry! Our brains were leaking after the bites they received!
Models featured include Bailey Ledford, Carol Moraca, Mel Heflin, Janelle Powers, Dedd Fredd, Jeff Joslyn, Charley Hayes, Bailey Marie, Dixie Lee, Candy Carnage, Dick Carlier, Catherine Moon, Jim Bevins, Dalton Brown, Janet Brickhouse, Mike Mayhugh, Jon Brown, Kyle Dickman, Rose Tennison, Natasha Smith, Zach Cousino, Heather Nance, Freddie Novak, Dani Danger, and more!

Written and compiled by Paul Burke.
Designed by Joshua Werner.
Edited by Paul Burke and Joshua Werner.

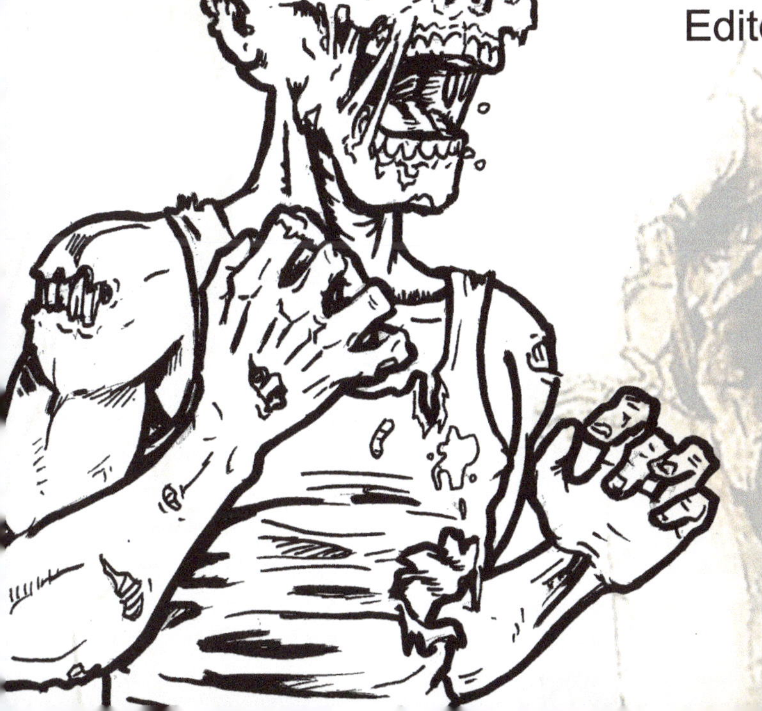

ASYLUM
PUBLICATIONS, INC.

www.ingramcontent.com/pod-product-compliance
Lightning Source LLC
LaVergne TN
LVHW070202110826
845147LV00002B/479

9781733930901